"What kind
of family draws
in an innocent
kid and makes
him the target
of murderers?"

ESPERS

THE DEAD OF NIGHT

THE

39

CLUES

PETER LERANGIS

SCHOLASTIC INC.

NEW YORK TORONTO LONDON AUCKLAND
SYDNEY MEXICO CITY NEW DELHI HONG KONG

This book is dedicated to
het snoper how anc loves eth deco.
— P.L.

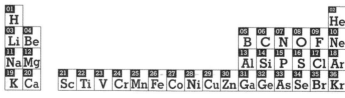

Library of Congress Control Number: 2011937771

ISBN 978-0-545-32412-0

10 9 8 7 6 5 4 3 2 1   12 13 14 15 16

Book design by SJI Associates, Inc.
Book illustrations by Keirsten Geise, Charice Silverman, and SJI Associates for
Scholastic. Lizard p. 131: © Lana Langlois/Shutterstock; hostages p. 131: Ken Karp and
James Levin for Scholastic; astrolabe p. 170: © Ivy Close Images (RF)/Alamy.

Library edition, March 2012

Printed in China 62

Scholastic US: 557 Broadway • New York, NY 10012
Scholastic Canada: 604 King Street West • Toronto, ON M5V 1E1
Scholastic New Zealand Limited: Private Bag 94407 • Greenmount, Manukau 2141
Scholastic UK Ltd.: Euston House • 24 Eversholt Street • London NW1 1DB

01 H																	02 He
03 Li	04 Be											05 B	06 C	07 N	08 O	09 F	10 Ne
11 Na	12 Mg											13 Al	14 Si	15 P	16 S	17 Cl	18 Ar
19 K	20 Ca	21 Sc	22 Ti	23 V	24 Cr	25 Mn	26 Fe	27 Co	28 Ni	29 Cu	30 Zn	31 Ga	32 Ge	33 As	34 Se	35 Br	36 Kr

CHAPTER 1

In all his eleven years, Atticus Rosenbloom never imagined he'd die on a bed of fresh rolls and sticky buns.

Of course, he never imagined being tied up, shoved into a sack, thrown into the back of a bakery truck, and taken on a high-speed tour over every pothole in the Czech Republic, either. If he needed any proof that hanging out with Amy and Dan Cahill was trouble, this was it.

"Wohogashamee?" he shouted. It was the best he could manage for "Where are you guys taking me?" with a bandanna pulled across his mouth.

It was no use. They couldn't hear him.

He fought back desperate tears. This had to be a mistake. They must have wanted some other nerdy kid with dreads, a plaid shirt, and beat-up Vans.

He jerked his body left and right, trying to loosen the ropes around his wrists. His head banged against a row of metal shelves. Breads and pastries cascaded to the floor, their sweet, yeasty smell seeming to mock him.

"Careful with the crullers, will you?" came a taunt from the front seat. "We may need them on the flight."

Atticus froze. He knew the voice.

His brain, which had absorbed eleven languages already, did not forget distinctive sounds. Or near-death experiences. Like yesterday's, when Dan and Amy lay trapped in a locked, burning library. Atticus and his half brother, Jake, had tried to help, only to be attacked by a woman and a guy dressed in black.

A guy with the same voice as this cruller-loving kidnapper.

Dan said they were killers. Twins. Vespers.

Suddenly, the whole thing was making some awful sense.

He knew Dan and Amy were Madrigals, the elite branch of the world's most powerful family, the Cahills. The Vespers were bad guys who had kidnapped seven Cahills. As ransom, Dan and Amy had to perform nasty tasks — breaking into museums, stealing ancient artifacts, solving impossible codes. Which they were capable of doing, because they'd found something equally impossible called the 39 Clues.

So why did the Vespers gas Dan and Amy in a library? And why do they want me?

Nuts. The whole thing was nuts!

The truck veered abruptly to the right. Atticus slid on a layer of raspberry jam and banged against the rear door.

As he screamed in pain, the truck came to a

sudden stop. The door opened and a pair of hands untied his sack. In a moment, Atticus was squinting against the sudden sunlight. The *whoosh* of a jet engine nearly knocked him over.

"Sorry for the bumpy ride," his abductor said, yanking the gag out of his mouth. "The next will be smoother."

Atticus's eyes quickly adjusted. The guy was maybe in his twenties. He looked like he'd wandered off the set of a magazine shoot for *Travel + Leisure*—blond, blue-eyed, tanned, and buff. Atticus could feel the rope being untied from his hands and replaced with a handcuff on one wrist behind him. A silky female voice added, "How many boys your age can say they've been on a private jet—for free?"

"I'm not a boy!" Atticus blurted, the words spilling out of his mouth faster than he could think. "Okay, chronologically, yes, eleven years old fits the definition, but in actuality, I'm a college freshman. So if you're looking for a boy, you've made a mistake!"

The woman came around to his side, her wrist now cuffed to his. "Just because we're holding hands, college boy, don't get any ideas."

Atticus recoiled from her clammy grip. She was unmistakably this guy's twin, but with the blondness cranked up to eleven. Her baker's uniform had extra-long sleeves to hide the handcuffs from sight.

"We don't make mistakes, Atticus," the guy said. "We know you won the county fifth-grade chess championship, and the state spelling bee on the word *renaissance*. By the way, I always had trouble with that word —"

"Let me go right now or I'll scream bloody murder!" Atticus shouted.

The man grabbed Atticus by the shirt collar. "If you scream, little dude, there *will* be bloody murder. And with that one hundred seventy-five IQ, you're too smart to put your brother and father in danger."

Atticus tried not to panic. The bits of knowledge — the cruel taunts — were like pricks of a tiny knife blade, keeping him off balance.

The man looked away briefly, checking his reflection in the window of a tan-brick building nearby. He ran his fingers carefully through his hair. "You babysit, Cheyenne. I'll run ahead to see that the jet's ready."

"Make it quick, Casper," his sister said, pushing Atticus forward. "And be sure there are enough mirrors on board for you."

"Your names are *Casper* and *Cheyenne*?" Atticus managed.

"And our last name is Wyoming. Want to make something of it?" Cheyenne yanked his wrist, picking up the pace. "We'd planned on giving you a meal, a parachute, and a safe landing. We could always forget the parachute."

"Wh-what are you going to do with me?" Atticus asked.

"We're taking you to a more secure place," Cheyenne

replied. "For a few questions. A simple transfer of . . . guardianship."

The blade twisted.

Atticus had always taken pride in being different. In being one of a kind. But there was one aspect he'd trade in a nanosecond.

He could still hear his mother's words on her deathbed: *I am passing along Guardianship to you. . . . You must continue. Tradition. So much at stake.*

All he knew was that Guardians fought the Vespers. And that he was the only one left.

"I—I don't know anything about Guardians!" Atticus said.

"Maybe you'll change your mind when we're through with you," Cheyenne said.

Atticus's legs wobbled. "What if my mom died before she could tell me anything?"

"I'd say that was pretty bad parenting," Cheyenne said with a shrug.

Atticus's panicked eyes scanned the airport. In minutes they would be on a plane, speeding away from Prague. He would be Hostage Number Eight. Caught by two Vespers who had already tried to gas Dan and Amy.

The Wyomings would think nothing of whacking Atticus Rosenbloom.

Think, Atticus. It's the one thing you're good at.

Casper was barking orders to a gray-haired airport worker at a hangar fifty yards beyond the tan-brick building. Cheyenne was pulling hard, trying to walk faster.

Atticus hated holding hands with this creep. The last female he had ever held hands with was his mom.

Mom, who was the kindest, smartest woman he ever knew.

Mom, who was a Guardian. Who told him in her last breath to *stay friends with Dan Cahill.* Who knew trouble was ahead.

Guardians were mixed up with the Cahills. Mom must have known something like this would happen. She had been taking precautions for years. She had secret papers. A weird tech guru on retainer.

Beezer.

The name popped like a flash of neon out of an inky mental cloud — Max Beezer, Mom's tech guy. Atticus and Jake had found tons of his little gadgets after Mom had died. Max had turned most of them over to Mom's assistant, Dave Speminer, but he had saved some of the cool ones for Atticus. Like the miniature tracker that he and Jake had been tinkering with yesterday. Neither of them was sure how it worked. It was nanotech. Weird design, way too tiny.

But worth a try.

He needed a moment alone. With his key chain.

Frantically he felt in his left pocket, but the chain was gone. He slowed down and moaned deeply, doubling over.

Cheyenne glared at him. "What?"

"Nothing. I'm okay. Really." Atticus convulsed again. "All those pastries on the truck . . . plus motion sickness. Bad combo. But I'll be f-f-fine."

"Oh, great—" Cheyenne stopped.

Casper's voice bellowed from within: "What do you mean, the plane isn't ready? Hello? Earth to old guy? We paid you in advance."

Cheyenne rolled her eyes. "Don't ever treat your elders like that if you grow up." Glancing toward the battered men's room door, she said, "This isn't a stupid trick, is it?"

Atticus gulped down some air. "I'll just"—breath—"sit next to you on the plane"—breath—"and hold it in."

"No, you won't." She pushed him toward the men's room door, kicked it open, and immediately blanched. "Ucch. That is the grossest thing I've seen in my life."

"I don't mind." Atticus pulled her inside, but she yanked back.

Reaching into her pocket, she took out a set of cuff keys and unlocked him. "You have two minutes. And don't try anything funny, or you will be so sorry."

Atticus peered into the bathroom and grimaced. "I need my key chain. So I can use my disinfectant."

"Your *what*?" Cheyenne said.

"My Germ Away," Atticus replied.

"What kind of eleven-year-old boy takes disinfectant into a men's room?" Cheyenne snapped.

"A clean one?" Atticus offered with a shrug. "It's just that . . . well, *you* see the sink and the toilet. . . . I mean, we'll be handcuffed together and all. . . ."

Cheyenne's face was turning green. She reached into her pocket and pulled out Atticus's enormous key ring. It contained seven keys, five plastic store rewards cards, a screwdriver, a flash drive, and a tiny but festive-looking can of Germ Away. She carefully examined the ring, item by item.

Atticus held his breath.

A slow smile crept across his captor's face as she held up the flash drive. "Ooh, clever boy. A transmitter!" She unhooked the drive, dropped it to the ground, and crushed it beneath her boot. With a triumphant, malevolent grin, she handed the key ring to Atticus. "Welcome to the big leagues, where IQ runs a distant second to street smarts. You have two minutes."

Atticus's jaw dropped. He cast a forlorn glance at the shattered pile of plastic and steel on the ground. As he turned to the men's room, he fought back a sob.

Slamming the door behind him, he flicked on the light.

One minute and fifty-four seconds.

He turned the sink taps all the way. Brown water gushed out loudly into a stained basin. He moaned. He could hear Cheyenne calling out to her brother.

Atticus held up his key ring, separating out the small can of Germ Away. Carefully he twisted open the cap.

It beeped.

Fingers shaking, he tapped an app on the tiny screen. And he began typing a code into the keypad.

CHAPTER 2

"Honestly, you *stood* there while they took the boy away?" asked Ian Kabra.

Amy shrank into the hotel room sofa. She felt numb. On Dan's laptop, Ian's features were exaggerated, his eyes wide and accusing. Behind him was the gleaming high-tech Cahill headquarters in Attleboro, Massachusetts, which Amy had designed. Once upon a time, Ian's dark, dreamy eyes had made her melt inside. The angle of his head, the wrinkle in the left corner of his lip—they'd obsessed her. And he'd been obsessed right back.

Now all Amy wanted to do was throw her shoe at the screen. She hated him. She hated his tone of voice.

She hated that he was right.

Reagan Holt, Ted Starling, Natalie Kabra, Phoenix Wizard, Alistair Oh, Fiske Cahill, and Nellie Gomez—seven people she cared about were festering in a jail cell. And now Atticus was gone.

What kind of family leader lets those kinds of things happen?

"Yeah, that's exactly what they did," Jake Rosenbloom blurted out, pacing the floor. "Nothing!"

"It's my fault." Amy glanced at her brother, who was curled up on the sofa in the fetal position. "Just me. Not Dan. I should have seen this coming."

On the screen, Sinead Starling elbowed Ian aside. Her red hair was pulled back with a rubber band, her delicate features taut with urgency. "I've alerted every Cahill in the area, our contacts at the Prague police, the Czech embassy, airports, limo services, every bakery from Pilsen to Hradec Králové. Nothing yet. I'm thinking the Wyomings used a private jet. Short flight, no conspicuous-looking fuel drain."

"They told me not to call the police!" Jake fumed, as if Sinead hadn't said a word. "Then they shoved me into a cab and took me here! Some family you have—thieves *and* cowards."

Amy bit her lip. She wished she *could* have called the authorities. But she and Dan were wanted for stealing a world-famous Caravaggio painting called the "Medusa," at the demand of Vesper One. Jake himself had turned them in to Interpol. Police were the last people they could afford to see now.

"Coming to us was the right thing to do," Sinead said. "We'll find him. We have the resources."

"What if you can't find him?" Dan's outburst startled them all. He looked up from his smartphone, his eyes streaked with tears. On his screen was an image of a skinny kid with dreads and a goofball smile. Atticus.

Amy ached for her brother. It hadn't been easy for Dan to make friends after the Clue hunt. He'd survived a collapsing cave, been helicoptered to the top of Mount Everest, become trapped in an Egyptian tomb, watched a man die in Jamaican quicksand, and been entrusted with a complex five-hundred-year-old formula. What other kid could relate to that?

Atticus could. He was the only one who really "got" Dan.

"I jinxed him . . ." Dan murmured. "It *is* my fault."

Jake's breath caught in his throat. He let out an explosive moan, more animal than human. A sound impossible to hear without becoming physically ill.

Amy knew what it felt like to fear for your own brother's life. She had been lucky. Dan was alive.

And she felt guilty she hadn't shown Jake the text message Dan had received from Vesper One:

```
You had Il Milione all this time. You
really shouldn't keep secrets from me.
Your punishment this time: A Guardian
goes down.
```

Despite all her training, she'd been caught totally unaware. Because she and Dan had been making a drop, and drops were always safe.

I should have been watching Atticus like a hawk. How could I have been so stupid?

As much as she'd wanted to tell Jake about the

note, she couldn't. Jake was a powder keg. He hated the Cahills and he'd betrayed Dan and Amy once. If he did it again, it meant jail time. Which meant death to the hostages.

And no hope for Atticus.

"This is about that Guardian nonsense, isn't it?" Jake said, nearly spitting his words. "Atticus's grandmother guarded some ancient map, which you guys stole from the library. My stepmother must have guarded something, too. Tell me, what was it? And what was Att supposed to be guarding?"

Amy replied with the truth. "We d-d-don't know," she said, fighting back the stammer that kicked in whenever she was bottoming out.

"And neither does he," Jake said. "So whatever this secret unknown thing is, it must be . . . unguarded. Am I right?"

Amy shook her head helplessly. "M-maybe."

"So whoever wants it wouldn't want the Guardian to find out about it," Jake barreled on, his voice rising in fury. "Because then he would go and guard it. So these Vespers . . . it would be in their interest to . . . to kill . . ."

Logic. Stupid, cold, awful, cruel logic. Stop it!

"They're lying!" Dan blurted out, his words sounding hollow and desperate. "That's what they do best. They said they would kill a hostage, too. But they didn't."

"They shot someone in the shoulder," Jake said. "That's close enough!"

Amy winced at the memory of the hideous footage of Nellie Gomez, their onetime au pair and now legal guardian, writhing bloody in the hostages' secret location.

Sinead's voice blared from the laptop. "Our operatives found a suspected Vesper command center in Legnica, Poland. Former Tomas territory. We've got the place under surveillance. Atticus could be there. So could the hostages."

Jake turned and bolted for the door. "I'm out of here. I will find my brother if it kills me. And if it does, I will take you all down with me."

Amy raced after him. "Jake, you can't!"

"'Sup, Attleboro-o-o-o?" came a loud stadium cheer from the monitor. Despite the fact that the image was mostly cap, sunglasses, chains, and radiant smile, there was no mistaking the face of world-famous rap artist Jonah Wizard. "Yo, my homeys, listen up—okay, my boy Hamburger and me? We're waiting here in Roma so long I'm afraid my cover is going to stop working. Do you know how hard it is to hide from fans in a country where my sales are through the roof?"

Jake paused for a moment, startled. He turned briefly to the screen, giving Amy just enough time to dart between him and the door.

On-screen, someone was bumping Jonah from the side.

Despite his muscle-packed, two-hundred-pound physique, Hamilton Holt had a hard time jostling Jonah for screen time. "Sorry, dude, but it's grub time and I'm wasting away. What Jonah means to say is, we were supposed to meet Erasmus, but he didn't show up."

"You guys are related to Jonah Wizard?" Jake asked, his lip curled disdainfully.

"And the other guy," Dan grumbled. "Vin Diesel's stunt double."

Jonah pushed his way into view again. "Yo, also? My man, Mac and Cheese? He didn't show up, either."

"He means McIntyre," Hamilton clarified. "Is this a lawyer thing, to miss meetings?"

"That's not like him," Sinead replied. "Or Erasmus."

"Did you say *McIntyre*?" Jake said. "As in *William* McIntyre?"

"You know him?" Jonah asked. "Skinny guy, a little dusty, nose like a screwdriver, kind of boring?"

"Yeah, I know him," Jake replied. "He's my dad's lawyer. And he's tough. Anything happens to Atticus, I will get him to sue you blind."

Amy took a deep breath. McIntyre was their confidant and friend, the man who set the hunt for the 39 Clues in motion. He had been there in the background, watching over them, like the eyes and ears of their late grandmother Grace. Painfully formal, he was the last person in the world who'd appreciate being called Mac and Cheese.

He was also the last person who would ever sue Dan and Amy.

"Sit, Jake," she said firmly. "This is more complicated than you think."

Dan shut the bedroom door quietly behind him. No more noise.

Enough of Jake's anger. Enough thinking about what happened to Atticus. One more moment and he would split apart.

He needed hope. Now.

He pulled his phone out of his pocket and checked his most recent text:

```
Suspend  judgment.  The  whole  story  is
always more complex than its parts. Wait.

AJT
```

The words made his blood race. The sight of those initials: AJT. The initials of his long-dead father. Arthur Josiah Trent.

Dan had only known him by the stories Amy told. By a blurry face in a tattered photograph he'd lost in the Paris Métro. AJT had died in a fire nine years ago. A fire that consumed his house and both of Dan's parents.

When this message came in, Amy had scoffed. *It could be anyone.* Which was logical.

But life was not ruled by logic. If the 39 Clues had taught Dan one thing, that was it. Sometimes good was bad, sometimes dead was alive.

Dan poised his thumbs over the keypad. There were so many questions he could ask to prove the ID.

Then, if AJT did prove to be real, Dan could ask him . . . well, everything. Whether Erasmus's tale was true — that Dad had been recruited by the Vespers as a young man. That Dad had renounced them, married Mom, and become a Cahill. He could find out how Dad had miraculously survived the fire.

But Dan's thumbs were frozen. The truth terrified him. Either way.

If AJT wasn't his dad, hope would be completely lost. Somehow, if you didn't know the truth, the possibility stayed alive.

But if he *was*, how could Dan adjust to his father coming back to life? Could he forgive the lack of contact? What kind of man would let his own son think he was dead for nine years?

And how could Dan deal with a father who was a Vesper?

Suspend judgment. . . .

Dan's eyes filled with tears. Images raced through his mind — helicopter blades cutting the cable of the gondola in Zermatt. The sight of Nellie, bloody and pale. The boat chase that had nearly killed them on Lake Como, and the halon gas in the library in Prague.

"Suspend judgment for what?" he murmured under his breath. "For nearly allowing your own kids to die?"

No. He couldn't complete this circuit.

He tossed the phone into a corner. It bounced harmlessly on the rug. That was exactly how he felt—harmless. Powerless. Tiny. Confused.

He was tired of being the helpless kid. The victim. The chased. The lackey for a voiceless Vesper. When would it stop? Why could they never be on top—why was it that *he* never scared anyone?

It doesn't have to be this way. . . .

Numbers and symbols spilled from his memory—a complex set of ingredients and precise formulas. It was the life's work of their ancestor, Gideon Cahill. A formula thought to have been destroyed in 1507, discovered in a cave in Ireland, and now known only by Dan. It granted superhuman abilities. Strength to overcome any attack. Speed to move great distances. Intelligence to outthink an army.

With it, every decision was clear. Every enemy was doomed.

Every mystery yielded to utter clarity.

Cheyenne and Casper Wyoming wouldn't stand a chance. The mystery of AJT would be resolved.

Dan wouldn't wonder if he had a father. He would know. He would know whether he was the one thing he wanted to be, more than anything else.

A son.

A son to the most detestable man in the world.

Twenty-six more ingredients. That's what he needed. He had thirteen of the difficult ones already—myrrh from a Chinese herbalist, iron solute and a solution containing tungsten ions from a machine shop, amber from a jeweler, iodine from a pharmacy, and a bunch of stuff from various chemical suppliers: mercury, liquid gold, zinc, magnesium, phosphorus, sulfur, calcium carbonate, and soluble silver in the form of silver nitrate. Some of the others, like water, clover, salt, and cocoa, would be easy.

"Dan, what are you doing?" Amy's voice suddenly called from the doorway.

Dan jumped. "Come on in, the door's open, thanks for knocking."

"I wanted to talk about Jake," she said softly.

"Oh, great," Dan grumbled. "Mr. Congeniality."

"He's so angry all the time. I can't bring myself to show him the text from . . ." Amy's eyes locked on the phone, resting on the carpet. Its screen glowed with the text from AJT. She sighed.

Dan scowled. "Here comes the lecture."

She sat on the floor next to him. "Dan, Dad was a Cahill. Through and through. Even if he wasn't born one. I wish you could remember his eyes. When you were little, he'd hold you up to everyone and say—"

"'Moon face,' yeah, I know, you told me a billion times," Dan said.

"You both would flash this big, identical grin," Amy said. "Mom said you were twins separated by a generation. The man wasn't capable of evil. His life was not a lie. If you really knew him, you'd *never* say the names *Vesper* and *Arthur Trent* in the same breath."

"People lie, Amy," Dan protested. "People pretend—"

"Dan, there were two bodies in the fire," Amy insisted. "No one could have lived through that. Besides, if he were alive, he'd be with us. He wouldn't have stayed away from the Clue hunt. He would have *led* it."

Dan spun around. "The bodies were burned beyond recognition. They could have been anybody. Uncle Alistair survived a cave collapse, Amy! Cahills do things like that. And if Dad tried to save Mom, then watched her burn to death—in a fire set *by her own family*? Because Isabel Kabra thought they were hiding one of the thirty-nine clues? You think he'd just be a happy Cahill after that?"

Amy's face drained of color. "What are you saying, Dan?"

"Remember Grace's note—the one we found after discovering the secret to the clues?" Dan said. "She said the Cahill family was broken. Untrustworthy. Isabel set the fire, and no one helped out—the Holts, Uncle Alistair, none of them. I'm saying Dad would have seen them for what they are. Murderers."

Amy's face darkened. "So you think he went over to the dark side, just like that?"

"He would have seen it the opposite way, Amy," Dan said. "The dark side was what he left."

Amy reared back her hand to slap Dan. He reeled in shock.

Before she could move, a beep sounded from Dan's smartphone.

They both froze.

Dan stooped to pick up the phone and noticed a blinking icon across the top of the screen. A GPS signal. He opened the app and saw a signal moving across a map of western Europe. Its origin was RUZYNĚ AIRPORT, PRAGUE. It was moving east.

Along the bottom was the name A. ROSENBLOOM.

CHAPTER 3

"Wake up and smell the limestone," said Cheyenne Wyoming, yanking the blindfold from Atticus's face.

He blinked. On the plane, hours earlier, he had lined up his worst fears — torture, plane crash, poisoning, being shoved out at thirty thousand feet.

Waking up at Site Number Seven on his Cool World Travel Wish List would not have been anywhere near the top.

Awestruck, he stared into a scene of lopsided, cone-shaped mountains, like giant castles made of dripping wet sand. "We're in Göreme, Turkey?" he said, his voice still froggy from a forced sleep.

"You're familiar with this dump?" Cheyenne said.

"In actuality," Atticus said, "it's one of the most interesting geological formations on the planet. If I weren't with you, I'd be running around like, *woo-hoo* —"

Casper pushed him hard. Atticus stumbled forward, his sleepy eyes focusing. His brain suddenly connected with something that had been dulled by sleep.

His terror.

Bread truck. Sack. Handcuffs. Jet. It all rushed back.

They had knocked him out on the plane. Cheyenne insisted on it. She was afraid he'd get sick.

He glanced around for a way to escape. He was no longer handcuffed, but there was nowhere to run. It looked as if they were in a vast moonscape, the monstrous rock formations casting deep shadows in the afternoon sun. He'd seen photos, but in person they were much bigger — like giant rock fingers poked through with enormous holes. Caves.

They were heading toward the largest rock, shaped like a sinking ship. At its base, an ominous-looking sign had been tied to a trash can:

DİKKAT!
ÇÖKÜK MAĞARA

Atticus rubbed his eyes, recalling his years of online language tutorials. "Wait, that's Turkish," he murmured. "And it means 'Danger: Collapsed Cave.'"

"Don't believe everything you read," Cheyenne said.

She shoved him in before he could protest. He hit

his head and had to duck low to fit through. His ankle twisted as it landed between two wooden planks, rotted and termite-eaten. Cheyenne scampered on ahead, waving a flashlight.

"I can't see!" Atticus said.

"Casper, where are you?" Cheyenne called over her shoulder.

"Emptying my pockets." Another flashlight beam, behind Atticus, began illuminating the planks. "A trash can outside. All the convenience of home."

Atticus stumbled along, his head scraping the low ceiling. "Wh-where are you taking me?"

"To a place where we can talk in private." Cheyenne stopped short. She gestured into a corner of the cave, sweeping aside a thick spiderweb. "Go."

Atticus peered into the pitch darkness. The cave seemed to end there, a tiny, dank chamber big enough for one person. Nothing beyond. Just a cranny in a cave where a dead body could rot and no one would ever see it.

Cheyenne pushed him in. As his back hit the cragged wall, she and her brother crowded close to him. A light blinked on above, bathing them all in a greenish white glow. "Unrecognized DNA," a mechanical voice droned.

"Allow access!" Casper called out.

A series of beeps was followed by "Voice recognition accepted."

The ground rumbled. With a loud scraping noise,

the floor beneath their feet began to move. They were on a circular platform, slowly sinking.

"No!" Atticus reached for the lip of the floor, but Casper batted his arms away. Bright lights flickered on below their feet, and soon the cramped, stinking cave gave way to a vast underground chamber.

The place was freezing. Enormous maps spanned the walls. A news ticker scrolled headlines near the ceiling. A bank of clocks ticked in unison, telling time in different parts of the world to the thousandth of a second. Brushed-steel cabinets lined the walls near empty computer workstations, their black, webbed chairs gathering dust.

The platform reached the chamber floor with a dull *thump*. Casper grabbed a chair. "Make yourself at home."

Atticus sank into the chair, sending up a small cloud of wispy dust. His throat was dry. He had to swallow twice before he could eke out a sound. "What am I supposed to do?"

Cheyenne pulled a handkerchief from her bag and dusted off two seats. The twins sat. "Tell us what you know."

"About what?" Atticus asked.

Cheyenne glanced at her brother, rolling her eyes. "The genius thinks he's too smart for us nincompoops."

"About being a Guardian!" Casper exploded, lunging forward.

Atticus screamed. His leg dug reflexively into the

floor, propelling the chair backward. He crashed against a computer table, the impact knocking the wind out of him.

Casper cracked up. "Brave kid."

"I suggest cutting to the chase," Cheyenne said, looking brightly around the room. "No one can hear you in here. No one knows where you are. You will not leave until you answer. And you will not live if you don't."

"I don't know anything!" Atticus insisted. "I told you! My mom was dying. She said I was a Guardian. She said we were enemies of you guys. The Vespers. She said you were after some secret. It was all in fragments—I can barely remember."

Casper grinned. He stood slowly and sauntered to the wall. There, he opened a cabinet door. "Maybe we can change that," he said.

Inside were a series of long knives. Casper pulled one out, a thin blade that made a high-pitched *shhhhink*.

Atticus felt the blood rush from his head. For a moment he could see only white spots. The room around him seemed to shrink, its frigid temperature warming, the walls rushing in, everything decaying into a tiny trap. . . .

His brain flashed an image of the tiny room at the airport. A men's room. A tiny can.

Germ Away.

"I know! I mean, I don't know!" he blurted, words propelling through his mouth before he could think. "That is, in actuality, I don't *know* the information. In my head. But I have it. All of it. That's how we Guardians do it. Even though we're, like, nerds and geniuses, all we know is the inscription."

Casper cocked his head. "The what?"

"Encryption!" Atticus said.

Slow down. Think.

Casper came closer, casually sliding the blade along his fingernail and shaving off a thin slice as if it were butter. "Go on. . . ."

"It . . . it's a precaution," he said. "To avoid hypnosis. And torture. And truth serums. We just know the key sequence, that's all. So we can decrypt it."

Casper flung the blade's tip forward, sending a fingernail into Atticus's face. "What. Exactly. Is it. *That you decrypt?"*

"It's all in my flash drive!" Atticus said.

Cheyenne looked dismayed. "The one I smashed under my foot at the airport?"

"No!" Atticus shot back. "Another one. Hidden on my key chain."

Casper's face darkened. He lifted the blade carefully over his head. Then, with gritted teeth, he hurled the knife at Atticus.

Atticus screamed and ducked. The blade tore through the fabric of the seat and impaled itself into the table behind.

"That's for making me have to go and get that stupid key chain," Casper said. "I threw it in the trash can outside. It was ruining the hang of my pants."

As he left, Cheyenne walked over to the bank of clocks. She stopped near one that said EASTERN STANDARD TIME, US, which read 7:02 A.M.

"This is Boston time, set precisely by the atomic clock," she said. "All your little friends are waking up and getting ready for school. In a half hour, at seven thirty-two, they will be running for the school bus. And you, halfway across the world, will have decrypted your flash drive and given us all your supposed information."

Atticus was shaking too hard to agree.

A half hour?

Even if he could make contact—with anyone—a half hour was not enough time. "I—I—m-m—"

"Chill out," Cheyenne said. "You're among friends."

"I may need more time," Atticus blurted out. "I need to . . . write code."

"It's a fast computer," Cheyenne drawled.

"But I'm a human," Atticus said. "Not even Mark Zuckerberg can code that fast!"

Cheyenne walked to the table where the knife was lodged. She yanked it out and held it toward the light. "Well, then . . . epic fail."

CHAPTER 4

"I don't care about pecs, lats, or smelts," said Natalie Kabra. "I am boycotting push-ups."

"Smelts are fish," said Reagan Holt, who was conducting a workout with Ted Starling, Phoenix Wizard, Alistair Oh, and Fiske Cahill in a dank cell. "What you meant to say was—*I want GOOD push-ups, people . . . thirteen . . . fourteen*—what you meant was *delts*. As in *deltoid muscles. Seventeen . . . eighteen.*"

"I *adore* fish," Natalie said with a dreamy sigh. She turned and banged on the cell door. "Excuse me! Hello—wherever you wretched people are? A little sushi down here? I'm wasting away. *Look at me!*"

Nellie Gomez closed her eyes and counted to ten. She had been looking at Natalie way too much. All of the rest of them, too. It was no fun to be stuck in these tiny cement rooms with one kid who couldn't see, another who barely talked, a fitness nut, a former burrito maker, and the winner of this year's Ichabod Crane look-alike contest. They were getting sick, too. All it took was one cold, and they were all infected.

Only germs could thrive in a place like this.

"Yo, Nat, ask for tempura," Nellie said. "With wasabi on the side. To clear the sinuses."

She shuddered with a sudden wave of pain. Joking wasn't so easy anymore, either. Everything above the neck hurt whenever she spoke. Being shot in the shoulder was the Number One worst event in her entire twenty-two years. Followed close by Numbers Two through Four: being away from gourmet cooking, giving up her iPod cold turkey, and enduring Natalie Kabra.

Natalie glared at her. "Were you trying to make a joke?" she said with a flip of her black hair. "Warn me next time, and I'll pretend to laugh. Even though mockery is awfully inconsiderate toward someone who saved your life. Oh, and by the way, you're welcome."

Nellie didn't have the energy to answer. Yes, Natalie had pulled the bullet from her shoulder — but only after she'd been forced into action. Her precisely plucked eyebrows made her the hostage with the most tweezer expertise.

And Natalie had been been fishing for compliments ever since.

"Come on, Alistair, sixty is the new thirty — give it to me!" Reagan shouted. *"Twenty-six . . . twenty-seven . . ."*

"Argghhh . . ." Alistair Oh collapsed, his once-green prison uniform now a grimy gray. Next to him, a thin, silver-haired Fiske Cahill also hit the floor. "I'm afraid our delts aren't what they used to be," Alistair said.

"Actually, mine rather *are* like smelts," Fiske

added. "Small and floppy."

Ted's arms were also wobbling, and Phoenix let out a loud sneeze. "Reagad?" he said, his voice nasal and clogged. "Baybe that's eduff for today. We're gettigg codes. We deed rest."

"We'll rest when we're dead, Wizard!" In a whirlwind, Reagan quickly knocked off fifty more push-ups, flipped, and did thirty crunches, then turned and landed a kick that dented the metal door. "I'm feeling sick, too, and look at me. What if Babe Ruth had said 'Time to rest'? Or Michael Phelps? Or Neil Armstrong? Come on, guys—what are we?"

"Hungry," Natalie said.

"Sleepy," Alistair added.

"Grumpy," Fiske said.

"Sneezy," Phoenix piped up.

"Shot," Nellie said.

Reagan was about to launch into another pep talk when Ted held up his hand. Nellie adored Ted. He'd been blinded in the explosion in the Franklin Institute, and afterward had become subdued and thoughtful. He didn't demand attention much, but when he did, he had good reason. Now he was sitting bolt upright.

"'Sup, dude?" Nellie whispered.

Instead of answering, Ted fell to all fours. "Shoulder to shoulder," he said softly. "Keep it close. Hunch."

It was an order. Cringing at the pain, Nellie dropped beside him. She eyed the ceiling cameras. Ted clearly wanted to hide something.

In the dust of the prison floor, he scraped in tiny letters:

THEY ARE DIRECTLY ABOVE US.

"We know that," Nellie whispered.

I MEAN, <u>CLOSE</u>.
I CAN HEAR THEM LAUGHING.

A couple of seconds later, he rubbed the words out.

Good, Nellie thought. This was new info. New info always helped.

Ted had developed an awesome sense of hearing since he'd lost his eyesight. He'd heard voices in the prison before, but never had he located them so precisely. She wasn't sure how this helped — yet. But that's why you became a Madrigal. To use info to your own advantage. She'd had a lot of practice with that.

"Dude, thanks," she whispered.

"Well, then, they can hear me just fine," Natalie said, angling her head upward. *"Request to food personnel! Send extra soy sauce!"*

Nellie stood and clapped her good hand over Natalie's mouth. Shrieking in surprise, Natalie stumbled backward and fell. "You pulled out my bullet," Nellie said, "but you're not going to sabotage us."

"That is assault and battery!" Natalie cried out. "I shall contact my barrister!"

"Back off, Rambo," Reagan said, pulling Nellie away. "Martial arts training begins next week!"

Nellie felt pain shooting through her whole body. *Bad move, girl.*

She hadn't meant to hurt Natalie. The dirt, the close quarters, the pain — they did something to her head. It was only a matter of time before the hostages began to lose their humanity.

Fighting back the agony, Nellie sidled over to the whimpering Kabra. "Sorry, Nat," she said. "When we get home? Sushi dinner on me, at my culinary school. But you gotta promise me one thing, okay?"

Natalie looked up warily. "What's that?"

Nellie put her fingers to her lips. "Stay quiet."

Wiping away a tear, Natalie nodded.

Taking Ted's hand, Nellie spelled out *How far?* with her finger on his palm.

Ted traced two vertical lines on her palm. *Eleven.*

Nellie knew what he meant — *eleven feet.* She eyed the dumbwaiter door. It was shut tight. The captors had been using the little elevator to convey food and fresh laundry. Up until now, the Cahills had no idea from how far up the stuff had come.

But now they knew they were just a few feet away from their tormentors. On the other side of a thin ceiling. Connected by a dumbwaiter. A dumbwaiter on which they'd already tried to stow away, unsuccessfully.

No, not a dumbwaiter . . . that's not how the floors are connected.

An escape idea began to form in Nellie's brain. While in culinary school, she had also been taking an art course. Her teacher had taught her that art wasn't only about the objects you painted. It was about the spaces between them.

"No secrets, please, Gomez," Reagan said. "We're a team."

Nellie shushed Reagan and drew everyone into a huddle again. She looked carefully from eye to eye and began mouthing words silently:

Reagan tried the dumbwaiter, but not the shaft.

Vesper One felt it again. The itch. How odd.

Over the years, he had weaned himself from touching the scar. There was no reason to. It was old, completely healed. The urge to scratch was merely psychological. Brought about on rare occasions — like the incompetence of his inferiors.

we have g, the message from Vesper Six had read. Nothing more.

That had been nearly a day earlier. Nothing since.

Have was such a word of cowardice, he thought. Especially when he was expecting the word *killed* to follow it.

The Guardian should have been dead by now.

If he isn't, someone else will pay the price.

Vesper One smiled, considering all the delightful possibilities. The itch, magically, was gone.

CHAPTER 5

7:29:52.

Atticus could barely see the screen. Sweat dripped into his eyes, stinging, blurring his vision. He had a good glimpse of the contents of his flash drive.

What he didn't have was a clue.

"Two minutes," Casper said, looking up from a phone game.

Meaning twenty-eight minutes of nothing.

Atticus's fingers clacked away. Down here the Germ Away transmitter was useless. But there had to be a connection to the outside world. The clocks were connected to the atomic clock. Which meant there was a network connection—satellite, wired, *something.*

"One minute . . ."

Atticus felt Casper's breath on his shoulder. For twenty-nine minutes, he hadn't shown a bit of curiosity, and now he was staring at the screen.

Atticus minimized all windows. "I need more time!" he blurted.

"Forty seconds . . ." Cheyenne said.

"Ten more minutes!" Atticus shouted. "Please!"

"What are you hiding?" Casper asked. "Let me see your work!"

Don't panic.

"I can't show it," Atticus lied. "Not yet."

"He's lying," Cheyenne called out. "He's trying to get a network connection."

"He wouldn't be that stupid," Casper said. "If he'd tried, he would have knocked out the system! *Let me see it!*"

"Twenty seconds . . ."

Not panicking was not working.

I'm dead.

"I don't know anything! I have been telling you the truth!" Atticus saw someone's fists banging on the keyboard. It took a moment to realize they were his own. Windows flashed across the monitor like uncaged bats. He felt his arms grabbed from behind.

"Time's up," said Cheyenne.

"He's got nothing," Casper replied.

"Fine," Cheyenne said. "Kill him."

⁘

Nusret Kemal did not mind driving a taxicab. Most of the people were friendly, and the work was pleasant enough. But as he drove into the arrivals section of the airport, his hands were shaking. He pulled up to the curb and left his car in the taxi line. Slipping the dispatcher a tip, he made a quick run inside for a cup of Turkish coffee and some sweets. To settle his nerves.

The last ride had been too bizarre for his taste. The robust American couple with their nervous nephew. What a family! The boy didn't look a thing like them and hardly said a word. The aunt and uncle—could anyone be so rude? Such a long ride, all the way to the caves of Göreme. They'd barked at him the whole time. As if he were a slave.

"A bad ride today, Mr. Kemal?" said the young lady behind the counter. She had a lovely smile.

"I have had better," he replied politely.

He was calming down. As Mr. Kemal stepped out the front door, he headed for his clean but slightly beat-up BMW.

It was pulling away from the taxi line with a squeal.

He dropped his coffee. "Hey!" he screamed, running as fast as his tired sixty-three-year-old legs could carry him. "Come back here!"

Too late. His car—his livelihood—gone! What was he going to do now? He fumbled in his pocket for his cell phone.

That was when he saw the envelope.

It was lying on the curb, where his car had been. He stooped down and picked it up. It was thick and sealed. Perhaps it would hold some clue to the thieves' identity.

He ripped it open violently.

A few people saw Mr. Kemal as he stood on the sidewalk, opening the envelope. Later they would say that his jaw nearly fell to the pavement with shock when he saw the wad of American money inside.

CHAPTER 6

Atticus felt a sharp blow on his back. He fell, hitting his jaw against the side of the desk.

"Harder, Casper," Cheyenne said. "Or do I have to do this myself?"

Casper crossed in front of the desk. He was holding a heavy flashlight, which had just made contact with Atticus's head. "Be right back, don't go away."

He gave the flashlight to Cheyenne and pulled open the knife cabinet.

Atticus bolted to his feet. The screen glowed up at him:

```
system operations aborting
activate fail-safe? y/n
```

Do something. Anything.

He thrust his arm forward and pressed Y.

The screen now showed a black background and a single line of text:

shutting programs . . .
one hour to self-destruct

Atticus backed away toward a sealed door. *What did I just do?*

The Wyomings were advancing on him. Casper brandished a long dagger.

"G-g-guys . . ." Atticus said. "L-l-look at the screen. . . ."

"Games are over, genius boy," Cheyenne said. "And don't even think of that door. It's locked tight."

I love you, Dad, Atticus thought sadly. *I love you, Jake. And you, too, Mom, wherever you are . . .*

An alarm sounded. The system's steady hum became a brief electronic shriek. And then . . .

BEEP.

The hum ended. There was a click, and the room went pitch-dark.

"What the—?" Cheyenne's voice rang out.

Atticus lunged forward, scoring a lucky hit to Cheyenne's abdomen. Both fell to the floor. Atticus grabbed her arm and bit hard.

"*YEOOW!*" she cried.

Atticus heard the flashlight clank to the floor. He stooped and picked it up.

He lunged toward the back of the room. Where was the door . . . ?

"*Stop him, Casper!*" Cheyenne's voice screamed in the dark.

Got it.

The latch turned easily. The electronic locking mechanism was out. Everything electric seemed to be out.

He bolted into a narrow, clammy stone corridor and flipped on the flashlight. His head smashed against a stalactite and he yelped.

Not good. That gave away his location.

He shone the flashlight once to get the lay of the land. Then he shut it off and plunged ahead. Hunched but fast. Careful was crucial, but speed was key.

Casper and Cheyenne were behind him in the room, stumbling in the dark, shouting, arguing. Atticus heard a crash. They'd knocked over something big.

As he sprinted, his ankles twisted in stone ruts. He flashed the light again. Ahead of him was a sharp fork in the rock. One path had to lead outside. It couldn't just be going to nowhere. Chances were that it circled around and met the path they had taken in. He tried to orient himself in his mind. He had always been good at that. Jake had called him a human GPS.

Left. No, right.

He raced up the right path, which led to an uphill slope—then another fork, and another. Now he was just guessing.

"Hey! Get back here!" came Casper's voice.

"You're heading into a trap!" Cheyenne shouted.

They're lying, he told himself. How far away were

they? Judging from the voices, maybe thirty yards. Close.

He glanced over his shoulder and ran smack into a stone wall. "OW!"

Atticus's voice echoed off the stone. He was at a three-way fork now. He stopped. No clue whatsoever.

"We heeeear you!" Cheyenne called out.

"Ready or not, here we come!" Casper taunted.

He chose the middle path and scampered as fast as he could.

It curved ninety degrees and then ended abruptly in a solid wall. Dead end. Not even a crawl space to hide in.

Casper's and Cheyenne's footsteps were loud. Close. Atticus felt sweat pouring down his body. His clothing clung to him. The cave was sticky and cold, and his hands were clammy. His flashlight slipped, hitting the ground with a loud *smack*.

He flinched. Standing stock-still, he stared at the passageway opening — back toward the nexus of the three-way fork.

The Wyomings' flashlights flickered on the floor there. "Did you hear that?" Casper said.

"Bats," Cheyenne replied.

Casper gasped with horror. *"You know I hate bats,"* he hissed.

"Bats bats bats bats bats," Cheyenne said.

"Stop it! We're not kids anymore!" Casper shouted.

"This way, Braveheart," Cheyenne drawled.

Casper's voice receded. To the left. "This is no joke. You should have been watching him. The system sensed an intruder. It shut itself down."

"Systems like this do not *shut down*, Casper," Cheyenne replied. "They self-destruct. Bats are the least of our worries. Blowing up would be top of the list."

The footsteps picked up speed, clattering away.

Blowing up?

Atticus waited, willing himself to breathe.

He caught a rush of cool air and sucked it in greedily. When he could no longer hear footsteps, he prepared to bolt.

But where? The Wyomings had clearly gone the correct way — but he couldn't just follow them. They'd be waiting for him.

He looked down, felt around for his flashlight, and bent to pick it up.

As his hand touched the metal, he froze. How had he been able to feel a breeze?

Caves didn't have breezes.

Unless . . .

He looked up. High above, he could see a line of wispy gray, like the ghost of some phosphorescent slug among the crags.

Escape equals breeze plus light, he thought, then modified the calculation.

Multiplied by impossible climb.

He had a sudden vision of his mom's face, all stern and exasperated. It was the day she'd signed him up, against his will, for rock-climbing lessons at the Brigham Recreation Center. He was afraid of heights. She had told him this was for his own good—which was what she also said about asparagus and chores.

He hooked the flashlight into his belt and grabbed a handhold above his head. *This time I gotta admit, Mom*, he thought, *you were right.*

The rock face angled slightly away, just enough for him to climb with foot- and handholds. Grunting, using muscles he hadn't accessed in months, he inched slowly upward. After about twenty feet, he climbed onto a platform.

In order to get to the light, he would have to make his way over a huge outcropping that angled above his head and was slimy with drippings—or crawl underneath it, through a rock tunnel about ten inches high.

He lay flat, squeezing through the opening. It was barely enough room, and he left shreds of his shirt on the rock floor. At the other end, just past the mouth of the passage, was a thin ledge. Atticus grabbed a fist-sized rock and threw it into the void. No sound.

He stood. Light seeped from above him, through a hole that was impossibly high.

Far below him came a distant *thook*. The rock he'd thrown had just landed. *How many seconds was that?*

He blanched. He couldn't think about it.

To get to the hole above, he would have to climb

a nearly vertical wall. He grabbed a handhold, but it came off in his palm and he stumbled backward.

His heel caught the edge. He wobbled, wind-milling his arms. At the last moment, he lunged forward again, grabbing another handhold.

This one held.

His heart juddered so violently he worried it would shake loose the rock.

Do. Not. Look. Down.

He tried again, keeping his eyes wide open. He made sure to test each jutting rock before shifting his weight. Slowly he made his way up the wall. The breeze washed over him from above, growing warmer the higher he got. It was wicking away his sweat. He could taste freedom. When he was within ten feet, he stepped up the pace, digging his foot into a deep hole.

His toe touched something that moved. A screech ripped the air. A tiny, black form skittered. Flapping its wings wildly, a bat flew at Atticus's face.

"Ahhhhhh!" he screamed.

He jerked his foot out. His left arm slipped out of its hold. He dangled by one hand, his shout echoing down the chamber. The fingers of his right hand slipped . . . slipped. . . .

He looked down. The abyss loomed black and large.

Desperately he lashed his left arm . . . over his head . . . back to the wall.

Got it.

His fingers latched on to the tiniest hint of an indentation. A rock dimple.

The bat flew upward, disappearing into the hole. Atticus swung his foot carefully into another foothold. He tried to stop from shaking. Shaking was not a help. His hands were wet. His feet felt numb. He looked down into the darkness but instead of seeing the pit, he saw his mom's face. *One foot after the other . . . this is how you overcome your fear. . . .*

He reached up again with his aching left hand. Up into nothing.

And this time he felt soil.

Digging his fingers in, he yanked himself up . . . up . . .

And then he was tumbling. Down a hill, through moist, sweet-smelling grass.

The sun was setting over the rim of a hill. He heard the distant bleating of sheep. The breeze ruffled his hair, and he smiled.

Standing upright, Atticus reached to the sky. A laugh welled up from the depths of his gut. It nearly exploded out of his mouth, rising and rising until it became a joyous, hysterical cackle.

And it stopped suddenly when an arm reached from behind and covered his mouth.

CHAPTER 7

Jake heard the screaming loud and clear.

Dan.

He ran toward the noise. The terrain was hilly, and they were now separated by a small ridge. He should never have let the kid out of his sight.

As he scrabbled up the rocky incline, his ankle twisted on a root. He crashed down hard, pain shooting up his leg.

Struggling to his feet, he thought about how much he hated Dan Cahill.

If it weren't for Dan, none of this would have happened. Atticus would be home, happily exploring dangerous places with Google Earth.

Not taken away by kidnappers.

He barreled over the top of the ridge, not seeing the other person hurtling toward him from the other side.

They collided at the top, and Jake saw black. He felt himself tumbling forward, down the other side, his limbs interlocked with someone else's. It wasn't until they hit bottom that Jake saw who it was.

"Att?" he said.

"Jake?"

Jake sat slack-jawed. The faint signal from Att's device . . . the race to the airport . . . the flight and the high-speed taxi ride . . . it was so fast. Like a dream.

But this was real. It all was real.

Atticus was alive.

Jake fell forward, forgetting the pain in his ankle. He wrapped his arms around his little brother, breathing in the familiar scent of Atticusness he knew so well, a combination of bubble gum and acne cream. "Are you okay?"

But his brother pulled away, eyes darting wildly behind him. "What time is it?"

"Huh?" was all Jake could manage.

"What time is it, Jake?" Atticus shouted.

"Almost five-thirty," Jake sputtered, "but—"

Atticus jumped to his feet. "We have to get away from here, quick—the Wyomings are right behind me!"

"The *who*?" Jake glanced behind. High on another sloping ridge, above a sheep farm, Amy was lifting Dan off the ground. "That's Dan and Amy, Att!"

Atticus's face fell. "Oh, no . . ."

"They set up this flight," Jake said. "If there were flight speed limits, we broke them. Then we took a taxi—I mean, actually *took* it—"

But Atticus was up and running, back toward Dan and Amy. *"I'll get them!"* he shouted. *"You run the other way, Jake! This place is going to blow!"*

The blast sent Dan flying. He landed on his shoulder and rolled down a grassy patch.

He spat dirt and sat up. As the dust settled, he saw shepherds in the distance, their sheep scattering frantically. But all Dan could hear was a tight, ringing sound. It was like a disaster film with the sound turned off.

Amy!

Where was she? He glanced around, squinting through the settling dust.

There. She was farther down the hill, groggy and dirty but safe. Jake was at the base of the next hill, and he looked okay, too. Atticus was between them, picking himself up from the ground. A moment ago, he had blindly flung Dan to the ground, thinking he was an attacker. Now he'd seen Jake. He realized the truth. He'd been rescued.

Atticus grinned as he saw that Dan was okay. He began running to him, his dreads flopping in the wind, his knees banging against each other. Dan couldn't help laughing. He had never noticed how skinny Atticus's legs were.

As Dan raced down the hill, his hearing began to return. He knew because he could hear Atticus's wild scream of joy. He grabbed his best friend, lifting him off the ground, swinging him in a circle.

"I thought you were Casper!" Atticus shouted.

x

"I should whap you upside the head for that," Dan said, "but I'm too happy!"

A moment later, Jake's arms wrapped around them both, then Amy's from the other side. With a big smile on his face, Jake was almost unrecognizable.

Atticus pulled away and let out another hoot of joy. "I can't believe you got my signal. I sent it from a men's room at the airport in Prague."

"It went dead during the cab ride here," Dan said. "We were petrified."

"That was when Casper took it from the trash can outside and brought it into the cave!" Atticus said. "This place was a Vesper headquarters. They were try-ing to pump information from me. Stuff about being a Guardian. I stalled and stalled, pretending I needed to use their computer. I guess I must have broken the system."

"Where are they—Cheyenne and Casper?" Amy asked.

"Didn't you see them come out?" Atticus looked back up toward the rubble. "I thought they'd be out before me."

Jake shook his head. "Nope."

Amy gazed at the debris, aghast. "They couldn't have survived that."

"I—I *killed* them?" Atticus said.

"Woo-hoo!" Dan shouted, raising his hand for a high five. "Good riddance!"

Amy shot him a look of shocked disapproval. "Dan!"

Dan shrugged. "It was self-defense. They were planning to kill him! Remember Vesper One's text—?"

Stupid. Big mouth.

He wished he could swallow back what he'd said.

"What text?" Jake said.

"It doesn't matter," Dan replied.

Looking Jake in the eye, Amy said, "We should have told you. Vesper One wrote to us. He'd found that we'd kept a secret from him. That's why he had Atticus kidnapped. He wrote, 'Your punishment this time: A Guardian goes down.'"

Jake's face went red with disbelief. *"This was a murder attempt on my brother?"*

"But Atticus murdered *them*!" Dan said.

"It wasn't murder!" Atticus squeaked.

Dan turned to his best friend. "Dude, don't worry about it. They're Vespers. They have no feelings."

"Sometimes I'm not sure Cahills do, either," Jake spat. He grabbed his brother away from Dan and began heading down the hill. "Let's get out of here. The car is behind the silo."

Dan lagged behind as the others jogged away.

He tried to summon up some sympathy for Cheyenne and Casper. He dug as deep into his soul as he could. But he came up with nothing. No feeling at all.

Dude, that's harsh. They were flesh-and-blood humans!

He'd had plenty of feeling when he saw Lester die in Jamaica two years ago. Dan had barely known the guy, but the horror haunted him to this day. Back when

Grace died, he couldn't sleep for three days. And forget about watching *Bambi* when he was a kid. Death was awful. For anyone. Even bad guys.

It was human to feel for others. Only psychopaths didn't have that capacity. Serial killers. Vespers.

Dan shook. Maybe, deep inside, he was like that, too.

Like father, like son . . .

As he walked, his ankle scraped against a scrubby plant and he jumped away. One of its buds, yellow and tightly round, came off in his hand. He recognized it immediately.

Wormwood. Swiftly he broke off a branch and stuffed it into his backpack.

Serum ingredient number fourteen.

It was like an answer. An omen.

With the serum, everything would make sense.

"Hurry, Dan!" Amy cried out.

The others were at the base of the hill. Dan raced after them. They all rounded the silo and ran to the stolen blue taxicab, parked in the shadow. It sported a coat of dust and some strands of hay stuck in the wipers. Jake reached into his pocket, pulled out the key chain, and pointed the infrared beeper at the car.

As it sounded, two figures rose up from the opposite side. One of them had a cell phone, the other, a pistol.

"Yes, Vesper One," Cheyenne said into the phone. "We have them."

CHAPTER 8

For dead people, the Wyomings had healthy smiles.

Amy edged toward Dan. The twins' rage radiated like nuclear waste. They were covered with soot, yet their eyes shone wildly. Casper's trigger finger was taut and white knuckled.

He'll do it.

Atticus's face was lined with confusion. "W-we thought you were crushed!"

"Oh, we were," Cheyenne replied, pocketing the phone. "The rudeness of cold-blooded eleven-year-olds can be devastating. But we got over it."

"I didn't do it on purpose!" Atticus blurted out.

Amy couldn't believe her ears. "Who are *you* calling cold blooded?"

Casper pointed the gun at her. "I believe, little girl, that you're on assignment from Vesper One. As are we. So why don't you complete your task, and we'll complete ours?"

He swung the gun to Atticus's face.

Jake grabbed Atticus and shoved him behind his

back. "You have to go through me first."

"Touching," Cheyenne said. "I'll buy hankies when they make the miniseries."

"We were having a debate," Jake said, meeting Casper's glare levelly, "about whether or not you were human. I believe I have switched sides."

"Don't provoke them, Jake," Amy said.

"Don't tell me what to do," Jake said.

"Good advice," Casper agreed. "See, Cheyenne and I were debating, too. About whether we needed armor-piercing bullets. And I won."

Jake's voice was low and steady. "He's not going to do it. Not this close. No human being is going to put a bullet through two brothers staring him in the eye."

Amy fought back her blind panic. Jake was desperate, buying time. Creating some kind of standoff. He was drawing Casper's attention to him alone.

It wasn't crazy. It was unbelievably brave.

We let Jake down. We told him Cahills were capable. Survivors. Strategists.

And now we have to prove it.

Cheyenne's phone jangled suddenly. Judging from the panic on her face, Amy knew who was calling.

"Shoot him now, Casper!" Cheyenne shouted.

Now.

Amy lunged forward. She snatched away the phone before Cheyenne could scream. Casper swung the gun sharply, pointing it between Amy's eyes. Jake tensed, ready to pounce.

Amy ducked, pressing the phone to her mouth. *"If Casper kills me, you will never get what you want!"*

Casper froze.

A soft, measured breathing came from the other end. Amy's skin ran cold. She was talking to *him*. Talking to Vesper One in person. Hearing his breaths.

Her hands could barely hold the phone. "Your headquarters is d-d-d-d—"

Stop that now.

"Destroyed!" she blurted. "And Atticus—the Guardian—is alive. If anything happens to a hair on his head and all four of us are not allowed to go free, we do not tell you what we found in the Marco Polo text—the next location! Take this deal or you lose!"

Amy exhaled hard.

Cheyenne and Casper stood gaping. For once, they were speechless.

Impressive.

Vesper One put his feet up on a polished oak desk. What a refreshing twist.

He had to admit, he'd been surprised to know she was heading the family. She'd never seemed the type. He thought she'd make his job easy.

But she was as canny as her brother. Smart. Strong.

This was going to be more fun than he'd thought.

He closed his eyes and let her voice remain unanswered. Silence was a potent tool.

What a difficult time it had been. The botched kidnapping. The Gomez shooting. The messy McIntyre affair. And now this. The Guardian was alive, Göreme Station was destroyed, and Vesper Six had failed. Six nasty little events.

Now the Cahills were holding back a location. And they had just given him an ultimatum.

Quietly he closed the phone. And smiled.

Amy heard a click on the other end of the phone line, and her blood seemed to stop. "He . . . hung up."

Cheyenne snatched back her phone. "Someone took her brave pills today."

"And washed them down with stupid juice," Casper added, cocking his gun.

But Cheyenne's phone beeped before she could put it in her pocket. Ashen faced, she held a text message to Amy. "You have mail."

Amy looked at in disbelief.

```
You win. The boy goes free.
```

She had to read it three times before it sank in. "We did it," she murmured. "We outwitted Vesper One!"

But more words were scrolling across the screen now:

```
Each good deal deserves another. Here's
mine. Limited time only:
```

1. You choose not to tell me the next location.
2. You go there without any instruction of what to look for.
3. I slaughter all the captives.

As Amy read them aloud slowly, Cheyenne and Casper smiled.

"What now, genius?" Dan said.

Amy took a deep breath. "He's bluffing. Cheyenne, send this text: 'Touch one hostage, and Dan and Amy Cahill disappear.'"

"Amy!" Dan shouted.

"Hey, it's your funerals," Cheyenne said, carefully tapping out the reply. "Enjoy the bloodbath."

Amy fought back a horrifying stab of doubt: Nellie, wan and weak with a shoulder injury . . . Phoenix Wizard, looking so vulnerable and innocent . . .

No. He needs us. We have something on him.

If there was one thing she'd learned during the last two years, it was to work from strength. To recognize the good fights. The Cahills had recognized her wisdom. They'd accepted her as leader.

A leader had one job. To lead.

She ignored Dan's bewildered look. Atticus's shaking.

In a moment, a message appeared on Cheyenne's phone:

Fair enough. The hostages live. For now.
Wyomings are to step away from the car.
Cahills have 15 seconds to give location.

Amy nearly collapsed with relief.

Jake pushed Casper aside and reached for the driver's door. "I was wondering, Cheyenne and Casper. Do you have a brother named Jackson Hole?"

In reply, Casper pressed his gun against Jake's forehead.

"Jake!" Amy shouted.

"We hear that joke all the time," Cheyenne said.

Casper chuckled. "You must think we're idiots. We failed Vesper One. We're as good as dead now. Do you think we care what happens to you?"

"What the—YEEOOOW!" Suddenly, Atticus leaped out from behind Jake, tearing at his own hair. *"Get them away!"*

"What is it?" Dan said, running to his friend. "What happened?"

"Bats!" Atticus shrieked. *"They're in my hair!"*

"Where?" Casper flinched, his eyes suddenly filled with fear. His elbow jammed against Cheyenne, throwing her off balance. *"Cheyenne, keep them away!"*

Jake rammed into Casper's midsection. Amy kicked Cheyenne away from the car. As Casper's arm swung up to hit Jake, she took it and bit down hard. Casper let out a yowl of pain.

The gun fell. Amy grabbed it before it hit the dirt

and pointed it at Casper. "That car," she said, "is now a Vesper-free zone. Move."

"Casper . . ." Cheyenne growled, "you are such a wuss."

Their faces twisted with pain, the Wyomings edged away. Jake slid into the driver's seat. Keeping the gun trained on Casper, Amy entered the passenger side, then so did Atticus and Dan. But as Jake started the engine, Cheyenne's phone beeped again. "Read it," Amy said.

Defiantly, Cheyenne thrust the screen forward:

```
Location?
```

Amy tapped out the answer with one hand:

```
Samarkand, Uzbekistan
```

"You told him the truth," Dan whispered.

Amy exhaled. "A deal's a deal. We don't want him to catch us lying."

As Jake revved the engine, another message began to appear, in chunks:

```
Kudos. But lest this seem too easy, let's
mix things up. Your next task: Find me a
stale orb. You have 4 full days, or say
farewell to a Cahill.
```

```
You pick.
```

```
If I don't hear your verdict in 30 seconds,
I choose.
```

Jake threw the car into park. "He can't be serious."

Amy's blood ran cold. "We can't pick somebody to kill!"

Dan banged his fist against the car armrest. "We can't match him. We can't outwit him. Every time, he just makes it worse!"

```
15 seconds till my turn.
```

Amy's mind was blanking out. Choosing a name would be impossible. Giving Vesper One the choice was even more impossible.

```
5 seconds.
```

Before she could decide, Dan grabbed the phone and typed two words. Amy saw them only for a split second before he pressed SEND:

```
Alistair Oh.
```

CHAPTER 9

Three sets of eyes glared at Dan like oncoming headlights. Atticus's jaw hung open.

Dan's thumbs stood rigid over the keyboard. He felt as if they were on fire. As if someone else had climbed inside his brain and pressed the keys.

What did I just do?

Amy struggled to get words out. "H-h-how could you?"

"Alistair . . . he's the logical choice. . . ." Dan said, searching for a train of reasoning in his brain. "The others . . . Nellie, Ted, Phoenix, Natalie . . . they're young. They have the most years ahead of them. Fiske is our uncle, too, Grace's brother. . . ."

"I can't believe this is coming from your mouth," Amy said hoarsely. "You're measuring the value of lives. That's not something for people to do!"

Cheyenne's phone, still in Dan's hand, beeped once more.

I will let the old man know who chose him

for this honor. I leave you to your search.
The clock starts immediately. 4 days.

Oops. 3 days, 23 hours, 59 minutes.

As Jake threw the car into gear, Dan tossed the phone back to Cheyenne.

"You can't just leave us here!" Casper demanded.

Atticus shrugged. "Watch us."

They took off with a screech of tires.

Dan stared out the open window, listening to the Wyomings' babble of protest recede. The breeze was hot and reeked of explosives. Devil's breath.

Four days. Ninety-six hours.

It was all that stood between an impossible task in a distant country and Dan's debut as a murderer.

The rain felt greasy on Jake's skin. He shut his window. In the distance, clouds sat heavily on the mountain-tops. Through a hiss of static, the radio blared some song that sounded like strangled, wailing cats.

Dan and Atticus were asleep in the backseat. Amy was nearly comatose in the seat next to him.

He knew she hated him. Fine. He could never forgive her for the things she'd done. Like the long delay in telling him about the danger Atticus was in. Like dragging him into the Cahills' dirty little string of international thefts and murder attempts.

What kind of family picks among themselves for someone to die? What kind of family draws in an innocent kid and makes him the target of murderers?

You'd think with all their money, they could pay for a little protection. And peace.

Jake suddenly snapped off the radio. "Hey, Amy, can I ask a question? Where do you get the money?"

"Excuse me?" Amy said.

"The private jet — you just made a phone call, and it was waiting for us," Jake said. "And that wad of cash you left the taxi driver when we took this cab? It was enough to buy a fleet. Where do you get it?"

Amy sighed. She longed to tell him the truth, but she had already revealed too much to the Rosenblooms. "From a contest," she said simply.

"Lottery?" Jake pressed.

"Not exactly," Amy replied. "Our grandmother Grace Cahill left every descendant a million bucks. Or they could give it up and instead join a hunt for thirty-nine clues leading to a secret. Family branches had been searching for centuries, fighting and killing each other. Somehow she thought Dan and I would unite the family."

"Because you're Madrigals?" Atticus said groggily from the backseat, stirring from his nap.

Amy nodded. "It was the only way the secret could be reassembled."

"So what was the secret?" Jake asked.

"It was destroyed, Jake," Amy said. "So it doesn't matter."

"When my stepmom died," Jake said, "she told Att she and he were Guardians. She also said she 'needed Grace.' Why? Is that what she was guarding from the Vespers — the secret of the clues?"

Amy shook her head. "I don't know."

This was upsetting Jake more and more. He tried to put the pieces together. But all he could see was Atticus, trapped inside a cave with those two blond maniacs. What if he'd been in there when the place blew up?

"How long does he have?" Jake asked.

Amy cocked her head. "Excuse me?"

Jake slammed on the brakes. The car fishtailed along the road. A driver honked loudly. Jake yanked the steering wheel to avoid a guardrail. Stopping on a grassy shoulder, he spun around to Amy. "What are you going to do for my brother?" he demanded.

Amy looked frightened. "What do you mean?"

"You're off to Samarkand," Jake said. "You've got an uncle to worry about. Some cockamamie secret to find. But the Vespers are out to murder my brother. *What are you going to do for him?*"

"I — I —" Amy stammered. She took a deep breath and looked out the window. "Jake, you and Atticus are going back to Rome. We won't be near you. But I'll make sure Attleboro keeps an eye on you. They have amazing coverage, Cahill agents in every country —"

Jake threw back his head and laughed. This was

insulting. "I see what Attleboro has done so far. The beauty contest winner, the posh boy, and the geek."

"Don't talk about them that way!" Amy snapped.

Jake leaned across the car. "Then don't talk to me about virtual protection. It won't work."

"What do you suggest?" Dan asked.

"It's not a suggestion, it's a demand." Jake spun around, throwing the car in gear. "My brother and I are going with you."

In a room with no decoration, a man and woman dressed in white looked up from a crossword puzzle.

The alert monitor was glowing red. Instructions, they knew, were to follow. Most alerts were code blue—mundane things, food and materials. Cost cutting.

Code orange was more difficult. Messy. Like the shooting of the girl in the shoulder.

Neither of them was expecting a code red.

They had taken bets on who they would kill first. The man had placed a hefty sum on the older gent who had come dressed in black. The woman had predicted the annoying athletic girl.

They leaned forward, suddenly intent as the name flashed.

"We both lose," the man said with a touch of sadness.

They had grown to like the Asian fellow with the cane.

CHAPTER 10

Due to added security precautions, all private charter flights from Kayseri Erkilet Airport are limited to account holders. All other reservations must be made in person.

Dan snapped his phone shut as he got out of the taxicab. He'd been trying for an hour to book a flight. For four.

He wished it were for three. Having Atticus along would be cool. Not so much Jake.

"I'll contact Sinead," Amy said. "She'll figure a way around this."

Atticus was grinning as he faced the airport. "Samarkand will be cool. It's the oldest city in central Asia. The name means either 'Fort of Stones' or 'City of Rocks' or 'Meeting Place.' No one knows for sure. But it was smack in the middle of the Silk Road route, where they transported stuff between China and the Mediterranean—thievery, intrigue, blood-

and-guts central. Genghis Khan went ballistic there and nuked the place. Well, not nukes, in actuality. More like beheadings, disembowelings, setting huts on fire, entrails strewn all over."

Dan felt his spirits lift. Amy rattled off history and put him to sleep, but Atticus made it sound interesting.

"We may end up taking the Silk Road," Dan said, heading toward the entrance. "I can't get a jet."

"What's that?" Amy asked from behind him.

"I said, *I can't get a jet*," Dan repeated. "They're requiring we book it in person."

"No, I meant what's that thing sticking out of your backpack?" Amy said. "The branch."

Dan swung the pack around. The wormwood branch had poked through a gap in the zipper.

He shoved it back in, hoping she didn't recognize what it was. "Must have jammed in there when I fell after the explosion."

"Sorry to butt in on the fun," Jake said, "but maybe one of us should run ahead and get in line?"

"Sinead says Interpol is tracking every flight out of Turkey," Amy said. "We can't take the risk. She says Dan and I will need fake papers and disguises."

Dan stepped up onto the curb and stopped. "How long will it take?"

"Tomorrow morning," Amy said with a sigh.

"Tomorrow?" Dan repeated.

The roar of an engine blasted from his left — and a

Harley-Davidson motorcycle with flame decals jumped the sidewalk in front of him.

A small crowd of travelers scattered.

"How do you say, 'You jerk!' in Turkish?" Jake asked.

"Erasmus!" Dan cried with relief.

Jake balled his fist angrily and shouted, *"Erasmus!"*

The driver pulled off his helmet and goggles, allowing his dark, curly locks to spill over the collar of his black leather jacket. The sun had created a raccoonlike pattern on his face. "At your service."

"Wait," Jake said, confused. "Erasmus is his *name*?"

Immediately airport guards surrounded the burly Cahill operative. He answered in his deep, firm voice — in their language. In seconds, they were walking away.

Dan watched in awe. "I didn't know you talk Turkey."

"I speak Turkish." The corner of Erasmus's mouth turned up slightly. His dark eyes seemed to dance. "My last name is Yilmaz. Originally from Istanbul."

"Sinead said you were missing!" Amy exclaimed. "Where have you been?"

The smile vanished. "We need to talk. Alone."

Dan looked sheepishly at Atticus. "A minute, guys?"

"You nearly ran my brother over," Jake said, glowering at Erasmus. "And this is your apology?"

"I'm deeply sorry," Erasmus said.

"Come on, Att," Jake grumbled. "Let's get a snack."

As they turned to go, Erasmus quickly parked his bike at the curb. Amy walked beside him, reporting what had happened. When she spoke about Atticus and Jake, Erasmus stopped. "What did you say?" he asked. "The younger brother is a *what*?"

"Guardian," Dan said. "His mother was, too. She knew Grace. Do you know what that all means?"

Erasmus exhaled deeply. "I am afraid our task with the Vespers is raising more questions than answers." He gestured grimly to a cement bench, in the shadow of a soot-stained column. "Please. Sit."

Dan felt a wave of fear. Normally Erasmus was all steely strength and confidence. But something about his expression was . . . off. Nothing obvious—just a bit of unsureness in the eye, a bend in his posture. His face looked haggard, as if he'd aged five years. "I am normally good with words. But they fail me now."

"Try," Dan said, fighting back the horrible possibilities. "Please."

Erasmus wiped his sunburned forehead with his sleeve. His voice was distant and halting. "I was in Rome. At a hotel. I wasn't expecting the door to be open. Someone had been there before me. By the time I entered the room . . . McIntyre was already . . ."

The sadness in Erasmus's eyes was enough to fill in the last word.

"No." Amy's face drained of color. "This is not funny, Erasmus. *Tell us this is some kind of joke!*"

"I'm sorry, children," Erasmus said. "He is gone."

A swirl of candy wrappers danced around Dan's ankles. He was glad to be sitting, because he didn't think his legs would hold him up. He heard a strangled squeak, and it took him a moment to realize it had come from his own mouth.

McIntyre . . .

It was impossible.

McIntyre had *been* the 39 Clues hunt. He'd set it in motion. He'd secretly watched over Dan and Amy—afterward, too. He'd been like a dad, teaching them how to paddle a canoe and keep a checkbook. He took them to the opera and didn't even mind if they slept. Together they'd cheered Red Sox homers and Patriot touchdowns. Like normal kids.

"He asked us to call him Mac. . . ." Dan said softly. The old guy was so formal. Hard as they tried, they could only call him Mr. McIntyre.

He wished he could take that back now. He wished he could take McIntyre back, and all the people who had done so much for him—Mom, Grace, Irina, Lester. They were all dead now. And the only ones left were Amy and . . .

Dad.

Suddenly, the faces washed out of Dan's mind, replaced by two stark words. As if they'd been seared into the folds of his brain by a hot iron.

Suspend judgment.

AJT's plea for understanding. For forgiveness.

Up to now, Dan hadn't understood the meaning. *What* was he was supposed to forgive? Now it was clear. The message had come in right around the time that Erasmus would have found the body.

He's asking me to forgive him for the murder of William McIntyre.

What kind of monster was he?

Forgive this? Then what? Who would be next?

The rest of the hostages. Erasmus, maybe. Amy. Until there's no one left. Just me.

Me and you, AJT. Is that the plan?

Just us?

Then one of us had better watch his back.

Dan whipped his phone out of his pocket and accessed his text messages.

"Dan?" Amy said tentatively. "What are you doing?"

"I'm saying good-bye," he said, "to a ghost."

The message glowed at him from the screen now, the words he'd read at least a thousand times. With a firm jab, he pressed DELETE.

Amy's eyes were full of tears. "Welcome back, Dan," she said.

But as she rested her head on his shoulder, Dan felt nothing.

Amy held tight to her brother. With McIntyre gone, it felt like they'd lost the glue that had held them together. Dan was rocking back and forth, his features hard and remote. Beside them, Erasmus sat with his head in his hands.

"Are you guys all right?" Atticus's voice called out.

He and Jake approached with trays of coffee, hot

cocoa, and bags of trail mix, chocolates, and chips. "I'm hoping this is a hunger issue?" Jake said.

"McIntyre is dead," Dan said, his voice flat and toneless.

Jake nearly spilled his tray. Atticus steadied him by the arm, and the two boys squeezed onto the bench. "What happened?"

Erasmus looked up curiously. "You knew him?"

"Since I was a little boy," Atticus said. "He was our family attorney."

"I had no idea." Erasmus bowed his head. "I am sorry to be the bearer of such awful news. And I promise I won't rest until I track down his murderer."

Jake looked dazed. "Why would someone want to kill him?"

"The information, alas, is of the utmost confidentiality." Erasmus glanced at Amy. "For that I would need clearance from . . . the very top."

Amy felt his eyes burning the side of her head. The idea — Amy, the very top — seemed so ridiculous now. McIntyre had died on her watch. Some leader.

McIntyre had always had confidence in her. Whenever she was full of doubt, he'd say, *There's really no other choice. You are born to that role, Amy.*

Well, he was wrong about that. She'd let him down on that score. At the very top of the Cahill family was a vacuum.

Amy shrugged. "Atticus and Jake are as far in this as we are. Tell them."

Erasmus reached into his jacket pocket and drew out two wrinkled sheets of paper. "Moments before the attack, McIntyre had been looking through files. He had procured a top secret Vesper list. When he sensed someone was coming, he hid it. He put up a fight, but alas, the attacker was swift and fierce. But as McIntyre died, he twisted his body in an odd way. He was pointing to the place where he'd hidden the papers—in his shoes. His attacker did not think to look there."

Kathmandu	Sierra de Córdoba
Pompeii	Delhi
Oakland	Araucania
Tonga	Manila
Kodiak	Istanbul
Quito	Nyanganu

"We don't know what this means yet," Erasmus added.

Amy was dumbfounded. The list made no sense. No geographical patterns. No obvious codes. Only one city name rang a bell.

"Pompeii . . ." she said. "The city was covered in pumice and ash after the explosion of Mount Vesuvius in A.D. 79. Grace wrote about Pompeii in her notes. She called the explosion the first test."

"What's that supposed to mean?" Erasmus asked.

"I don't know," Amy murmured.

"So go there," Jake said. "Do some research."

"I can help you book a flight," Erasmus suggested. "I have family in hotels, transportation. . . ."

Dan paled. "We can't, Erasmus. We need to get to Samarkand or Uncle Alistair will die."

"Jake and I can go," Atticus said.

"Over my dead body," Jake replied.

"You're not the boss of him!" Dan snapped.

"Then who is?" Jake retorted. "You?"

"Stop!" Amy said. *"Just stop it right now, all of you!"*

They stared at her in shock. In a split second, they would be back to arguing.

You are born to that role, Amy. . . .

Amy took a deep breath. "I didn't mean you and I should go, Dan. And I didn't mean Jake and Atticus, either. Erasmus, I would like you to contact Jonah and Hamilton and arrange to meet them in Pompeii. And I mean *now.* The four of us will wait for the ID papers from Sinead and travel to Samarkand. Erasmus can book us a hotel."

"Oh, and no one else has a say in this?" Jake snarled.

Erasmus raised an eyebrow. "Those sound like orders, don't they?"

Amy felt a tiny snag of doubt, but she pushed it aside. She met Jake's glance firmly. "Those are orders."

Erasmus smiled. "That's what I like. A boss who knows who's boss!"

CHAPTER 11

"Whoa, these are free?" Atticus said, digging his hand into a silver bowl of gourmet chocolates on the hotel reception counter.

Looking up from the desk, Amy sighed. He was just like Dan sometimes. "Knock it off, please, Atticus," she said.

"Since when did you become his mother?" Jake asked.

The receptionist eyed them all with a nervous smile. "Welcome to the Grand Nikia Hotel," she said, handing Amy a set of magnetic card keys. "You've got two penthouse rooms on the twentieth floor."

Amy took the cards and headed toward the elevators. Jake was storming ahead. He wasn't going to let her off easy — on anything.

She exhaled. What was with him?

His broad forehead, refined jaw, swept-back hair — all of it promised intelligence, wisdom, security. She had to admit he was gorgeous. A gorgeous, irritating bonehead.

She worried that letting the Rosenblooms come along might just prove to be a colossal mistake. Saving Uncle Alistair was going to be the hardest task of her life. And she would have to do it after losing a night in Turkey, with Interpol on their tails, a genius kid marked for death, and a hottie who hated her guts.

She crossed the hotel's enormous lobby, which had a vaulted ceiling and an ornate fountain. In the center was a bank of clear glass elevators in the shape of tubes, rising twenty floors and letting people off onto circular balconies. All the rooms opened onto these balconies, and Amy could see people coming in and out of the doors. Her eyes fixed on them as she walked.

Something didn't smell right to her.

As she stopped by the elevators, Dan plowed into her from behind. His head was buried in his smartphone. "Sorry, I'm working," he said. "I'm thinking that *stale orb* is an anagram."

"Well, think with your head pointed straight ahead, okay?" Amy said, looking around the lobby.

"Vesper One's note said 'Let's mix things up,'" Dan continued. "That's an anagram hint. Mix the letters up."

"Hey, there's a restaurant here," Atticus said.

"No restaurant," Amy replied. "We have a lot of planning to do."

"So what is Atticus supposed to eat, the dust balls under the bed?" Jake asked.

"I've been rearranging the letters," Dan barreled

on. "Want to know what I found? *A lobster.* Also *bat loser.* And *rat lobes.*"

"Keep working," Amy said. As the elevator door opened, she felt her phone vibrating. She nearly jumped.

She was feeling too edgy. That wouldn't be useful.

The screen showed Evan's name. "Hello, Ev?"

"Ames!" he squeaked. "We just heard the news from Erasmus. All I wanted to do was, you know, touch base? How's it going? Are you okay?"

For a moment, Amy felt a smile breaking the stalemate of expression on her face. No one said hello like Evan. He was a ball of sweet eagerness.

As the elevator door opened, she felt tears rushing to her eyes. It was refreshing to speak to someone whose first concern was her.

Crying?

Jake worried about the leadership skills of Amy Cahill. He watched her face carefully. She was talking to . . . what was his name? . . . Tolliver. From the video transmission in the Prague hotel. The nerdy guy. Her boyfriend. She was crying and smiling.

Funny. When she smiled, all the tension drained from her face.

She was really pretty.

And you're an idiot for thinking that. And, doofus, she's noticing you.

Jake turned away from Amy's eyes. He didn't

care, really. She deserved to have a boyfriend, like anyone else.

The elevator began to rise. Behind Jake, Atticus was helping Dan with anagrams. Amy finished her call and hung up. Jake noticed her eyes had changed. They were scanning the hotel skittishly.

What was she so nervous about? So many secrets in this family. So much paranoia.

"Slob rate!" Atticus exclaimed.

"I don't think that's it," Dan drawled.

"What are you toddlers yapping about?" Jake said.

Amy shushed him. She was staring upward. Jake followed her glance.

High above, a man leaned over the balcony. He was dressed in a black suit with no tie, a wide-brimmed black hat, and sunglasses. He was scanning the area slowly, as if searching for something.

"Why is that guy wearing sunglasses?" Amy asked. "The lighting scheme is dark. No normal person would need to wear those."

"A Turkish film star?" Jake suggested.

"He's on our floor!" Amy said. *"Someone hit the button. Any button."*

They were rising quickly—eleven . . . twelve . . . thirteen.

"Amy . . . are you okay?" Dan said.

Amy lunged across the elevator and pressed the seventeenth floor. The elevator came to a stop. "Get out—*everyone*," she said, pushing Jake by the shoulder.

"That guy is waiting for us. Up on the balcony."

Jake stumbled out. The girl was strong. "How do you know?"

Amy ran past him, onto the floor. She frantically pressed the button to an elevator going down. A door immediately opened. "Get in. Now!"

The elevator was crowded with other people. Amy shoved Jake and the others inside, then made her way to the glass wall.

"Amy, chill!" Dan urged. But his sister was fixated on the scene above.

Bewildered, Jake watched the man in sunglasses. He seemed to freeze as he spotted their descending elevator. Then he began walking quickly toward that section.

At the same time, the elevator in the tube next to theirs rose to his floor.

A young woman emerged. She also wore sunglasses and was dragging carry-on luggage. She grinned at the sight of the man, throwing her arms around him. Together they strolled away from the elevator and toward a hotel room door.

They were guests. Plain and simple.

"Hi ho the derry-o, the Vesper takes a vife," Dan sang.

Amy sank to the floor. "My bad," she murmured.

Atticus and Dan cracked up. Jake fought back a grin.

When the door opened at the lobby, the other bewildered passengers couldn't get out fast enough. They rushed around a stooped, balding man, who was smiling at Amy and Dan.

"Excuse to me?" he said in a thick accent. "Is you . . . Daniel and Amy Cah-heel? Friends of Erasmus Yilmaz? I am manager. His cousin Bartu."

Amy nodded. "I'm Amy, this is Dan."

The man's eyes watered. He grabbed Amy by the face and kissed her on both cheeks. "Any friend of Erasmus is family to me!"

Fool. Paranoid.

Amy breathed deeply, trying to slow her heart rate. She would have to stay cool. Leadership meant knowing when to be afraid and when not to. Alistair's life depended on not jumping to conclusions. On being alert but not stupid.

"Come, I have lovely gift—Erasmus pay for it!" Cousin Bartu said, hurriedly padding toward a door marked AUTHORIZED PERSONNEL ONLY in several languages. "Sorry, he did not tell me about other two boys. But I find something nice for them, too. You bring back. They will be happy for to get."

The Grand Nikia was the friendliest hotel ever. Any place associated with Erasmus had to be.

The old man led Dan and Amy through the door. They passed through a set of cubicles staffed with hotel personnel. Then he led them through another door, and an alleyway.

At the end of the alley, about twenty feet away, was a black car with tinted windows.

"Have a good day!" Bartu said. With a speed Amy never would have imagined in an old guy, he slipped back through the door and into the hotel.

"Hey!" Dan screamed.

Amy reached for a doorknob but there was none.

The car door opened and a burly, rumpled-looking man climbed out. He wore a shabby brown trench coat and a shabbier brown fedora, and the dark circles under his eyes suggested a habit of very little sleep. Amy recognized him right away.

"We . . . know you," she said softly.

"I believe you eluded me on a train to Switzerland," he said wearily. "But we have not formally met. Milos Vanek. Interpol."

Vanek.

That was the name signed to an all points bulletin to art dealers and museums about Dan and Amy's theft of the Caravaggio.

Think.

"We have a flight tomorrow. . . ." she said, walking toward him. "Please. If we don't make it, someone will die. Let us go. We're just kids."

"*Just kids* do not commit thefts of priceless art," Vanek said. "Come with me."

Amy saw the doors of the car opening. She lunged forward, leaping.

Her right foot made contact with the car door. It slammed shut on a set of fingers. A bloodcurdling cry rang out from inside the car.

Amy spun. Vanek had jumped away and was reaching inside his jacket pocket. Before she could react, Dan was behind him, quickly lifting the trench coat up over Vanek's head.

As Vanek let out a cry of surprise, Amy sprang forward. She pulled the bottom of the coat toward her. Vanek's arms, trapped by the sleeves, flew over his head, too.

He shouted in some unintelligible language, whirling around blindly, his coat inside out.

"Come on!" Amy shouted.

She grabbed Dan by the arm and ran.

A gunshot made her stop short. "Hands in the air and turn around!" a gruff voice shouted.

Behind her, on the opposite side of the car, an agent with thick beard stubble stood with a pistol pointed into the air. Vanek, frantically unwrapping himself from the twisted trench coat, threw it to the ground. He was facing the wrong way. As he spun to face them, his hair stuck out in all directions.

The gunman let out a strange, coughlike noise. He looked toward Dan and Amy, then Vanek.

Inside the car, the other agent climbed out. Seeing Vanek, he burst out laughing. The gunman joined in, both men soon screaming with hilarity at the sight. "I think you have your hands full, Milos!" the gunman said.

"No, my friend," Vanek spat, smoothing down his hair. "They do."

CHAPTER 12

Dan hadn't expected Interpol headquarters to be luxurious. But it looked like the walls hadn't been painted since the days of Caravaggio. Maybe since Medusa herself. Judging from the smell, that may have been the last cleanup time, too.

With Amy and Vanek, he reluctantly followed a lumpy, uniformed woman down a dark corridor. Her shoes, which looked like they weighed forty pounds, clomped loudly on the cement floor. She stopped at a metal-barred door. In the next cell, a prisoner yelled in Turkish, causing the guard to strike the inmate's bars with her key chain. The yells became piercing shrieks. "In, please," the guard said, opening the door.

Dan peered inside. The cell was unlit, the only illumination coming from a buzzing, greenish fluorescent light in the hallway. There were two bedlike structures, cement benches with thin mattresses thrown on top. "You can't mean this," he said.

He felt the guard's hand shoving him inside. Amy stumbled in beside him.

"We're entitled to a phone call!" Amy said.

"Ah, the phone call." Vanek shook his head sadly. "American demands. Just like the movies. Tell me something. You steal artwork of highest refinement . . . Renaissance treasures. Is it a game for you? Why? You intend to sell the Caravaggio on eBay?"

"We don't have the Caravaggio!" Dan said. "Someone took it from us!"

"Ah," Vanek said, leaning against the bars. "Who?"

"A trapeze artist," Dan explained. "But she was killed. And someone took it from her."

Amy shot him a look.

"I see." Vanek's eyes went dead. "You continue to believe that mockery is a sound strategy. Ah, well. In the morning, we will consult with officials in Turkey. They will consult with officials in Italy. They will consult with officials in United States. They will consult with Interpol. They will consult again with Turkey. Maybe in a week, maybe three, we will schedule a hearing."

As he turned to go, Amy shouted, "Three weeks? We have to make our flight tomorrow morning!"

"Someone smart enough to steal a Caravaggio can rebook a plane flight," Vanek said, without turning around. "Good night. Enjoy your accommodations."

Amy sank onto the bench bed. As the wails of the prisoner next door reached an intolerable pitch, she shoved her arms against her ears.

But Dan couldn't move.

All he could think about was another jail cell in

another place. Three days from now. He was picturing that cell's door opening.

And the look of utter horror on Uncle Alistair's face.

The dumbwaiter began to rattle.

Phoenix Wizard shook like a mouse in an ice bucket. He wasn't built to be a hero.

Reagan Holt had managed to pry loose two sturdy metal bars from a rickety bed frame. The poles were hidden in the shadows in another room. Nellie was throwing Reagan a thumbs-up. Everyone was trying to be upbeat.

Phoenix blew his nose and added his wet tissue to a pile on the floor.

This part is my idea. I don't HAVE ideas!

What if this failed? What if—?

A hand landed softly on his arm. Phoenix turned.

Nellie was grinning widely at him. *Love ya*, she mouthed.

As the dumbwaiter neared bottom, Natalie emerged from the other room. From under her prison garb, she pulled out the metal bars and gave them to Reagan.

The door opened, revealing a plate of stale bread and a plastic container of warm water.

Now.

Phoenix swept the contents onto the floor. "The eyes!" he shouted.

Fiske and Uncle Alistair both scooped up the wet tissues and began flinging them up at the surveillance camera. Their aim wasn't bad. One by one, the tissues stuck solidly to the lenses, blocking the view.

"The mouth!" Phoenix said.

Reagan and Nellie dragged a heavy bed across the cement floor. Phoenix pushed off the mattress, leaving a naked metal frame, which they shoved into the dumbwaiter sideways, jamming the door open.

The machinery groaned as it struggled to raise the contraption.

"The guts!"

This was the trickiest part. Phoenix joined Reagan and Ted, who were lifting the bed frame up, using it as a lever. The front of the bed frame pushed against the dumbwaiter floor, forcing it down.

Phoenix had figured there must be some clearance, some room in the shaft *below* the dumbwaiter. They needed the floor to sink about a foot and a half.

As the dumbwaiter floor slowly sank, he watched the roof. Above it now was a growing black space of about four inches . . . six . . . ten. . . .

"Now!" Phoenix shouted through gritted teeth.

Uncle Alistair shoved one of the bed-frame bars into the gap between the dumbwaiter roof and the frame of the wall opening. "Not . . . sure . . . this will hold . . . !" he shouted.

With a sickening *ping*, the metal flew into the shaft like a flicked toothpick. Alistair doubled over in pain. "My hand!"

The bed frame jerked down. Phoenix's heart

skipped a beat. "Keep pushing!" Reagan shouted.

Nellie and Fiske raced to his side. Their added strength allowed Phoenix to duck away and grab the other pole.

"You'll kill yourself!" Alistair warned. "The pressure is too great!"

Ignoring him, Phoenix reached into the gap. He stuck one end of the pole into a depression in the metal frame of the dumbwaiter. Carefully he slid the other end into a small hole in the wall frame.

It held. Barely.

The dumbwaiter began to vibrate violently. A coil of acrid black smoke rose from below.

And then the motor went dead.

Phoenix leaned his head into the gap and stared upward. A dull greenish-white light emitted from a wall opening about twelve feet above. "I see them!" he said.

"Go!" Reagan urged.

Gripping the dumbwaiter roof, Phoenix hoisted himself upward, into the darkness. He planted his feet on the roof and began shimmying up the elevator cable. He could see Reagan below him, following close behind.

Phoenix had never been able to climb more than five feet on the rope in gym class. It felt as if someone had plunged knives into his biceps. "I . . . can't!"

"You will!" Inches below him, Reagan managed to reach up with one hand, gather the soles of both of his feet, and give them a powerful shove.

Phoenix vaulted upward and tumbled through the wall opening and onto a cold tile floor.

He sprang to his feet, blinded momentarily by the fluorescent lights overhead. He was in a long room lined with file cabinets. "We did it, Reagan!"

Reagan jumped into the room, landing in a crouch. "Don't just stand there—get 'em!"

She raced past Phoenix. He blinked away the brightness. At the far wall, two people sat at a bank of computers, facing away from them.

Phoenix followed, his blood pumping. The people weren't moving. Now he could see over their shoulders, to the monitors. Each was divided into multiple views: the two prison rooms below. The corridor outside the cell. The dumbwaiter shaft.

His stomach sank. *They've been watching us all along!*

That was when he realized that another image on the screen was *this room*—Phoenix and Reagan running toward a camera like a mirror.

The two Vespers rose calmly and turned. They were wearing gas masks.

"Stop, drop, and roll!" Reagan shouted, throwing herself to the floor.

Phoenix nearly barreled into her. Plumes of smoke swirled out of gas jets in the wall, surrounding them both.

And all went black.

CHAPTER 13

"I smell sheep, no?"

The voice came from just outside the cell door, high-pitched and lilting. Amy opened her eyes and realized she'd fallen asleep. All she could manage was a groggy "Huh?"

A gray-haired woman appeared outside the door, silhouetted in the harsh fluorescent light. "You have been consorting with sheep earlier this day."

Amy suddenly remembered they hadn't had a chance to change since their encounter with the Wyomings. "Um, yes, sort of."

Dan rose from his thin mattress. He stared uncomprehendingly at the shadowy woman. "Don't tell me. The Ghost of Christmas Past?"

She opened a shapeless cloth coat and pulled out an ID card. "Amato," she said. "Luna Amato. Interpol. Perhaps you heard of me? I asked your friends to give you a message. A large boy. And one who is into the rapping music. No? Ah, well, no matter. We meet anyway."

Amy cocked her head curiously. The woman had a

brusque, matter-of-fact manner, but there was a glint of kindness in her eyes.

Or maybe that was wishful thinking.

"If you came to yell at us, too late," Dan said. "Milos Vanek beat you to it."

"I come to transfer you. I trust you will not miss these chambers?" Amato pulled a key and two sets of handcuffs from her coat pocket. She unlocked the door and cuffed herself to Dan and Amy. "Come."

She began walking down a long hallway, the opposite way from which they'd come. "Ms. Amato, my brother and I are innocent," Amy pleaded. "Victims of blackmail. I know it sounds far-fetched, but if we don't travel tomorrow, a family member will be murdered!"

She looked at Dan for support, but he looked hopeless.

Amy had to admit, the explanation didn't sound airtight.

Luna Amato led them silently through a door at the end of the hall, and then down a flight of stairs into a moldy cellar. The halls were narrow, lit by bare bulbs. Battered metal file cabinets lined the walls.

"Wh-where are you taking us?" Amy said.

"Andiamo," Amato barked, picking up the pace. She led them past a set of small offices and up a short flight of steps to a tiny metal door.

Amy was gripped with panic. *Solitary confinement?*

Luna Amato extracted keys from a hidden pocket, unlocked both cuffs, and pushed open the door. Cool air swept in. Moonlight shone through distant branches.

"Follow me quickly," she said. "Do not look back."

"Mrrrp?"

To anyone else in the Cahill universe, the high-pitched sound of the pet Egyptian Mau had a hundred different meanings: the playful *mrrp*, the I-want-red-snapper *mrrp*, the that-wasn't-enough-red-snapper *mrrp*, the thank-you-for-the-meager-portion-of-red-snapper *mrrp*. And on and on.

But to Ian Kabra's ears, each was the I-hate-you-with-all-my-soul *mrrp*.

As far as he was concerned, the feeling was mutual.

At least this time, the fickle feline was keeping a distance, behind him and blessedly out of sight. With Sinead taking a power nap and Evan off to do homework, he had the place to himself.

Well, almost.

"Mrrrp," the cat repeated, more urgently.

"Yes, Saladin, you're here, bully for you." Ian stared intently into the electron microscope at a scrap of Lucian stationery. It was his only souvenir from the horrid explosion in the DeOssie factory — an investigation into the manufacturing source of the Vesper smartphone. "Now waddle away, dear Marquis of Mange, will you? I'm busy."

Saladin coughed and made a sound like vomit. Lovely.

Oh, for the pets of his Kabra youth — each homing

poodle with its own small estate, each thoroughbred in a private barn with *Black Beauty* running on DVD all day. Back then, *Egyptian Mau* was the label on a fur covering for a thousand-dollar pillow.

Where it belonged.

He glanced briefly at the list of names. They matched a portion of the list found on the body of William McIntyre. This was a major find—could there be a connection between the Vesper secret and the Lucians? It seemed preposterous. Having grown up in the home of the branch leader, Ian knew all the family secrets.

By rights, he should have shared the scrap with the rest of the Attleboro staff. But he had kept it to himself—because of one name on the list, one city.

Araucania
Kodiak
Sierra de Córdoba

Some things had to be examined in private first. For dignity's sake.

He positioned the microscope over a nearly invisible speck. It was embedded in the carbon, and to the naked eye, it appeared to be a stray piece of ash. But something about this had caught Ian's eye. Now, after scrubbing it with art-restoration fluid and putting it under the microscope, he saw the dot's true colors.

Gold and red. Lucian red.

"Voilà," Ian murmured. He pressed a button, and a chart popped up on the computer — a list of every chemical in that tiny speck.

Liquid gold. Just as he had suspected.

And one other familiar substance: Its chemical profile matched that of nail polish. Lucian red nail polish.

Red polish with intertwining gold-leaf snakes.

"Dearest Mother," Ian murmured with a rueful smile. "Your fingers are in everything, aren't they?"

"MRRRRP!"

The cantankerous cat was twining around his ankle. Ian was not in the mood. He gave it a swift kick across the room before it could scratch him.

He quickly accessed the UN website. He would need to pay someone a visit, someone he hadn't seen since the hunt for the 39 Clues had changed his life.

His mother, Isabel Kabra.

As he reached for a pen to leave a note, the cat leaped onto the desk and deposited a dead mouse. *"Get that thing out of here!"* Ian shrieked.

But Saladin was already strutting out of the room, head high and hips swaying.

Looking away from the shredded little rodent, Ian took the paper scrap, turned off the microscope, and dashed off a note to Sinead on the back of an envelope — Gone to New York.

Then he left before he would have to get sick.

CHAPTER 14

Vesper Five extracted a long knife from a butcher block. It was rusted. Clearly it hadn't been sharpened in years.

Horrible. Such sloppy housekeeping.

With slow, steady strokes, the Vesper slid the blade against a whetstone. Each metallic *sssshink* gave a sharp echo in the small room.

The phone beeped, and Vesper Five put down the knife to read the message:

Have we achieved the goal?

Oh, dear. Vesper One was all about results. He had no taste for the art. The agent snapped the phone shut, put it in a bag, dropped it on a small table in the other room, and returned.

The knife glinted, like a winking eye. Vesper Five raised it high and brought it down on the warm flesh. A wet, satisfying *thump*. A clean split.

Life's tiny pleasures could not be denied. Vesper

One's answer would wait. Sometimes goals were best accomplished on a full stomach.

Luna Amato threw both halves of the chicken breast in a pan.

First, the children would be fed.

The shower water was rusty and smelled like sulfur. Dan had to touch an old-lady slip in order to untangle a towel from the rack. Luna Amato played Italian opera that sounded like the screaming of dying wildebeests, on a vinyl-record player that skipped. The house belonged to Luna's Turkish friend, who apparently had grown-up grandchildren, because Dan's "clean change of clothes" was a pair of baggy jeans and a musty *NSYNC T-shirt. He felt like a time traveler from 1999.

He desperately wanted to talk to Amy. They would need a plan of escape. Amato was Interpol. She would not make it easy for them.

As he transferred the contents of his pockets, Dan found his phone. He couldn't believe she hadn't taken it.

What kind of Interpol officer is she?

Dan quickly tapped out a text to Attleboro.

We r out of jl. In trky. Still w Intrpl agnt, L Amato. Vanek w be on tail. May need extraction.

"Daniello!" Luna's voice called out.

Quickly Dan pressed SEND. As he left the bathroom, the aroma of pasta sauce and garlic was overwhelming. "Wow, nice," he said.

Luna looked up from the stove, where a freshly showered Amy was helping out. Although his sister was silent, her eyes were broadcasting *Let's get out of here.* "Before I am Interpol," Luna Amato said, "I am Italian. A simple dinner while we discuss your future. Pasta. Chicken with rosemary. Do you like rosemary?"

Dan was about to sneer but stopped. Rosemary was a serum ingredient.

"Totally," Dan said. "I'm a huge fan."

"Take some," Luna Amato said, waving toward a pile of pine needle–like sprigs. "And take silverware to the table, too."

Dan gathered up forks and knives. He stuffed the rosemary into his pocket as he moved into the living room. Fifteen ingredients now. Twenty-four more to go.

The living room had a long wooden table and patterned wallpaper, faded with age. He heard a sudden tap from the window and nearly jumped.

It was only the rustling of branches in the wind.

"Do not worry, Vanek is not coming," Luna Amato called out. "He does not know I stay here."

Dan gulped. It was as if she'd seen him through the wall.

Within minutes, the table was groaning with steaming pasta, chicken, garlic bread, a salad with slices of ham and stinky cheese, and plates of olives and peppers and other pickled things Dan didn't recognize.

As fast as Dan and Amy could eat, Luna kept forcing more.

"Daniello, you do not like the bread? Eat! . . . *Per favore*, have some more *pasticcio di gnocchi alla boscaiola!*"

"As long as you don't ask me to repeat the name," Dan replied.

Luna Amato chuckled. "Charming boy."

"Handsome, too," Dan said.

Amy gave him a swift kick under the table.

Amato poured Dan another glass of grape juice. "You must dine fast before your sister gets the other ankle, no?"

Luna took a few bites, then wiped her mouth. "Ahh, *bene*, I finally have lost the taste of that prison in my mouth! Please forgive my mysterious ways. You must wonder why you are here, no? I will tell you. It is because of Vanek."

Dan looked at Amy. She had stopped chewing.

"Behind his back we call him Milos the Monster. I have seen him do things. . . ." Luna looked away and sighed. "Well, perhaps not a topic while we eat. I took you from him because I know the fate you would otherwise suffer."

"Thank you," Amy said. "But . . . what are you going to do with us?"

Luna looked at her sharply. "Were you telling the truth? About being blackmailed?"

"Yes!" Amy said. "We just . . . we're not at liberty to say why."

Luna nodded. She took a sip of water and adjusted her glasses. "I am not certain what to do with you yet. I will keep you overnight and decide."

She fell into a long silence, as if remembering something sad. Dan began counting wrinkles on her face but stopped. Something about the old woman seemed familiar. Not a resemblance, exactly. It had to do with the set of her jaw, the softness of her eyes. Her expression changed the atmosphere in the room. It said, *Take your time; I am listening*, but not in a squishy, aren't-they-cute way. She was someone who took you seriously. Even though she was the enemy, she made you feel like the most important person in the world.

Despite her plainness, rumpled clothes, and thick accent, Luna Amato reminded him — just a bit — of Grace Cahill.

Amy sat back in a padded armchair. Her stomach pressed against the waistband of her jeans. The dinner had been sumptuous, the conversation friendly. Now she and Dan were alone in the den before the fireplace, with hot cocoa and Turkish cartoons on TV. The lingering smells of the dinner made the room feel cozy and warm.

She looked over her shoulder. Luna was puttering

around in the kitchen, singing to herself. She had a sweet voice.

They were far enough away that she wouldn't hear them talking softly. Amy eyed the windows and contemplated an escape plan. Dan had told her he'd contacted Attleboro, although he wasn't sure they'd gotten the text.

Maybe it wouldn't be so hard to do this on their own.

"Luna's softhearted," she whispered. "Do you think we can appeal to her?"

Dan shrugged. His eyes were half closed. "Hey, Amy, is this what our house was like? Did we sit around and have hot chocolate and TV at night?"

"Sometimes," Amy said.

"All I remember," Dan said, "is that nine-inch black-and-white TV with Aunt Beatrice and her false teeth. Watching *Wall Street Week* and eating frozen dinners. Some family. Wouldn't it be cool to have a real one again?"

Amy nodded. She wished Dan could remember their old life. "When we grow up," she said, "we'll have amazing families. Our dens will be better than this. Your kids and my kids will play together in a humongous room with every kind of toy and game."

"Except I won't have kids," Dan said. "I'll come over myself and play. . . ."

"Are you having fun?" Luna Amato called from the

kitchen. "I must make a phone call. And then I will join you! I have a surprise!"

Before they could answer, Dan's phone buzzed in his pocket. As he read the text, his mouth fell open. "What the—*Amy, come read this!*"

She jumped across the room and looked.

```
V-5 is Interpol agent Luna Amato. Repeat.
V-5 = Amato. Reply at once.
```

Amy's field of vision went white for a long second. *Luna . . . a Vesper?*

"We weren't rescued," Dan squeaked. "We were kidnapped. Like Hansel and Gretel."

Amy grabbed his arm. "We're busting out of here—now!"

They slipped out of the den. Luna was chatting on the phone in the kitchen. On a table, Luna's pink cell phone was lit up, sticking out of an open purse.

"How can she be on the phone in there," Dan said, "if the phone is here?"

"She must be using a landline."

Dan dug in Luna's purse. "Car keys," he whispered.

Amy looked at the back door. They'd have to run past the kitchen and hope she didn't see them.

Luna was pacing now. Amy could see her moving shadow. "On the count of three," she whispered. "And fast. One . . ."

Luna's arm appeared in the entranceway. "I must return to my guests," she was saying.

"Two . . ."

The arm was gone, the voice receding.

"Three!"

They raced to the door. Amy grabbed the knob. It wouldn't budge.

"Heads up," Dan said. He took a heavy porcelain mug from the sideboard and threw it through the door's window. The glass shattered and he reached through to the knob outside.

"Dear heavens!" came Luna's voice. "What do you think you're doing?"

Dan snatched a massive pewter pitcher and hurled it at Luna. She twisted away, but not fast enough. The pitcher clipped her on the shoulder and she went down hard.

"Go!" he said. "Go, Amy!"

She raced through the door. Dan was heading for a blue car in the driveway. He tossed Amy the car keys. "Don't drive like you! Make it fast!"

Amy caught the keys and climbed in. Dan slid in beside her. "Okay, Hansel," she said, "how do we get to the airport? We didn't leave bread crumbs."

"Who needs bread crumbs," Dan replied, "when you have a GPS?"

CHAPTER 15

Nellie felt Phoenix Wizard's neck. His breathing was steadier now. She tightened the tourniquet on his right arm. When they'd thrown his unconscious body down the dumbwaiter shaft, the poor kid had landed on a metal gear. And then Reagan had landed on him. The sound of the impact had been awful.

Why did I let them do it?

Nellie went over the sequence of events. She could not get it out of her mind. It was a stupid idea. She and Phoenix had talked it over as if it could work. She had convinced herself it was brilliant. Foolproof.

And then she had allowed a twelve-year-old to climb into the belly of the beast.

"How are his wounds?" Alistair asked.

"Bad," Nellie said. "That was a hard fall. But thanks for ripping off your sleeve, Al. It's stopping the flow. He's going to need stitches, though."

Fiske leaned over Phoenix and swabbed his facial

scrapes with alcohol-soaked cotton. He'd stashed away some from when Nellie was shot.

"Owwww," Phoenix moaned.

Nellie winced.

"Can't you fix him?" Natalie said, curled up against the wall in a fetal position. "Must we hear him groaning in pain? *I can't sleep!*"

Nellie spun on her. "Will do, Nat. I'll tell Phoenix not to let his pain interfere with your beauty rest."

"Hey, at ease, guys," Reagan said, her voice breathy from an aching chest bruise. "I'll sew him up, good as new . . . push-ups again by Sunday."

"You can't sew him," Nellie said. "You broke your wrist!"

A series of odd clicks made her spin around. Ted had poked his head into the dumbwaiter's small opening. He was making the noises with his tongue.

What's going on with these people?

"Yo, Ted—I can bind a wound but I'm not so good with decapitations!" she shouted. "Get away from there!"

"I'm gauging the exact distance of Phoenix's fall, by listening to the echo of the clicking," he said, pulling out of the gap. "From the floor above to the roof of the elevator, I'm thinking nine feet and . . ."

He stuck his head back in. The pole, which was still holding the gap open, shifted. With a sickening groan, the dumbwaiter inched upward.

Ted's body twitched. His feet left the ground.

Nellie sprang to her feet and leaped across the room. She put one hand on the top of the dumbwaiter and pushed downward. With the other, she pulled Ted out of the hole.

He fell to the floor, gasping. The pole snapped, hurtling back into the room, end over end. It landed on the floor with a dull *clank*.

The dumbwaiter thumped upward, closing the gap.

"It's a good thing you couldn't see that, Ted," said Reagan.

Nellie's shoulder felt like it had been cleft open with an ax. She sank to her knees, screaming. All around her, faces blinked in and out of her vision.

"Dear girl, are you all right?" she heard Fiske ask.

"Nell, you're a hero," Alistair exclaimed.

A hero who sent a sweet kid to his possible death!

Tears streamed down Nellie's cheeks. You didn't get many chances in a place like this. You had to make them count. Not do anything stupid. Not harm others with an act you weren't ready to take yourself.

"Please . . ." she said with a grimace. "Just shoot me."

Alistair leaned close to her. "Nellie, come. You need to lie down."

"This is my fault," Nellie said.

"It was a calculated risk," Alistair said. "A brave one."

"Hey, we'll get 'em to fix the dumbwaiter like

new and send us supplies!" Reagan said.

"Are you crazy? They will not be taking requests anymore!" Nellie shouted. "Be real, people! Exercise will get us nowhere. Trying to outwit the Vespers with tissues and bed poles — comic-book stuff! Either we kill these clowns or they will kill us!" She turned her face to the ceiling. "Come and get us, you cowards!"

A dead silence fell over the room. Nellie's shoulder throbbed. She found herself wavering at the edge of consciousness.

Natalie uncurled herself from the floor. She stood, her eyes red and her face flushed. In a voice that seemed to well up from her toes, she shrieked:

"I want my mother!"

"Hurry!" Dan shouted.

"I'm going ninety." Amy leaned forward in the driver's seat, peering over the steering wheel in a way that reminded Dan of Aunt Beatrice.

The car jerked to the right, causing Dan's phone to slide off his lap. He managed to catch it, avoiding a hang-up on Sinead, who had placed him on hold while she confirmed their flight to Samarkand. "Ninety *kilometers*, Amy! That's like fifty miles an hour! And if you have to go slow, at least be smooth!"

"It's fifty-six miles an hour," Amy said. "It's also the speed limit. After all we've been through, we don't want to be stopped for a ticket."

"Hello?" came Sinead's voice over the phone speaker. "Are you all right?"

Dan held the phone between himself and Amy. "I'd probably get to the airport faster on foot. Were you able to switch the flight? Luna Amato knew the flight number! We told her! She's probably got word out to the Vespers."

"Dan, listen to me," Sinead said. "*Interpol* wants to stop you. The Vespers need you to get to Samarkand."

A realization settled over Dan like a cracked egg. "You mean . . ."

"Luna wanted you to escape," Sinead said. "That's why she sprang you from jail. She was *planning* to let you go."

"So we didn't have to do what we did. . . ." Amy murmured. "Great. Once again, they're pulling the strings. We get in trouble, they free us so we can run around for them and break more laws."

"At least we got a nice meal," Dan said.

"Your disguise and identifying documents will be given to you by an undercover Cahill, who will find you," Sinead replied. "You'll be boarding the nine twenty-one commercial flight as Shirley and Roderick Cliphorn."

"Roderick Cliphorn?" Dan groaned. Only someone with a name like *Sinead Starling* would have considered that normal.

As the two girls jabbered on, making plans to notify

Atticus and Jake, he stared out the window. It had started raining. In the pale streetlamp light, the trees looked like people dancing.

He thought about Amy's reaction: *We didn't have to do what we did.*

She was right.

They could have done more.

The pitcher was heavy, he thought. *I should have aimed for the area between the eyes.*

With Luna out of the way, the Vesper Council of Six would have been reduced by one. It would have sent the perfect message, right to the top of the Vesper chain.

For a moment, Dan spotted his own image reflected in the car window. Over the last few months, people had been telling him how much his face had changed, how much he'd grown up. Usually he hated that kind of talk. But in that window, he saw for the first time the shape of a face he knew only from an old photograph long since lost in the Paris subway.

He was beginning to look like his dad.

CHAPTER 16

Amy bolted around the corner and looked at the arrival screen. "Boarding in ten minutes. Come on, slowpoke!"

Dan was skulking along the wall, his wig's floppy red hair falling over his face. "You didn't tell me *I* would be Shirley," he hissed.

"It wasn't my idea," Amy whispered, pulling her brother close. Her hair had been yanked upward into a floppy cap, and her upper lip stung from the spirit gum holding a small mustache. "We had to match the fake documents Erasmus gave us. Look, if Vanek tracks us, we're in that Turkish jail till we turn thirty. So until we're in Samarkand, Shirley—"

"If you call me that name one more time," Dan said, "I will scream."

Amy grinned. "I think you look kind of cute."

At the gate, Atticus and Jake were scanning the small crowd frantically.

"Pssst, it's us!" Amy said.

Jake did a double take. "What on earth . . . ?"

Atticus let out a spray of lime-flavored Doritos.

Then, with a squeal of delight, he jumped on Dan, smothering him in a big hug. "We were so worried!"

Jake stepped toward Amy. She shrank back, bracing for ridicule, or a scolding for being captured. But he wrapped her in a hug. "Glad you're okay."

For a moment, Amy was stunned. As he drew away, Jake's face was neither mocking nor stern. He was smiling like a little boy. She'd never seen him like that.

Warily, Amy filled in the details of the last few hours. Atticus and Jake had been updated by Sinead, but they listened in rapt attention.

Jake shook his head as if he had been ripped apart by worry. "I had suspicions about that old guy at the hotel. I shouldn't have let him take you."

"It wasn't your fault, Jake," Amy said.

He looked at her, his eyes seeming to ask for forgiveness. Amy looked away uneasily.

But she didn't not like the feeling.

The boarding call for Samarkand echoed through the terminal. Dan started for the gate. "Let's go, Rod."

His phone buzzed a moment later, stopping him in his tracks. He pulled it out to read the screen.

Ashen, he turned it to Amy:

```
Enjoy your freedom, Shirl and Rod. It's
later than you think. And tell the dear
little Guardian to watch his back. I
never forget.
```

Amy's stomach knotted. "How does he always know?"

"'Later than you think'—what's that mean?" Dan asked.

"Maybe . . ." Atticus said softly, "he's already killed the hostages. . . ."

Amy caught Dan's eyes. The very suggestion was barbaric. Inhumanly callous. And exactly the kind of thing Vesper One would do.

"Ask him!" Jake urged.

"We can't," Amy said.

"Um . . . yes, we can." Dan reached into his pocket and pulled out a familiar-looking pink cell phone.

Amy was stunned. "You took Luna Amato's phone?"

"Sorry. I couldn't resist," Dan replied with a shrug.

Atticus hooted. "Shirley, you rock!"

Dan typed quickly:

'Sup, Vespy? Our turn for a demand. If u
expect to get next item, show us proof
that the hostages r alive.

They waited a moment in tense silence until an answer appeared:

Nice touch. Proof to come. But hurry. You
have 2 days and 5 hours. As for G, I'll
let the timing be a surprise.

CHAPTER 17

"Watch it, Amy!" Dan cried out.

Amy looked up from her notes about Samarkand, inches away from colliding with a barrel full of melons. As she stopped short, a woman carrying a box of red peppers detoured around her. The Siab Dekhkhan Market, just outside the hotel, was busy with shopkeepers setting up for the morning.

"Sorry . . . sorry . . ." Amy murmured.

They had arrived in the dark after a flight delay. Amy couldn't sleep and had started her research before sunrise. Till now, Samarkand had been a progression of the senses. In the dark, it was different aromas—warm bread baking in the wee hours, coffee brewing. As morning broke, so did a choir of sounds—prayer ululations, taxi horns, delivery trucks rumbling into the market. Daylight brought the sights of an ancient Muslim market—an ocean of colors from spice vendors.

She elbowed through the already crowded plaza in the shadow of the massive Bibi-Khanym mosque.

Its blue and gold tiles glinted impossibly bright in the sunlight. At this pace, she felt like one of the elephants that had lugged stone from India to build the massive structure. Vendors shouted offers of peppers, breads, rice, fruits—the best prices! She wanted to identify it all. To soak up every bit. But not now.

She looked around for Atticus and Jake, who had run on ahead to get a taxi. Dan lagged behind her, practically drooling over a display of disc-shaped breads that were flattened in the center. "Look, little naked pizzas!" his voice piped up.

"Sorry, Mr. Pokey, we're not stopping," Amy replied. "The observatory opens in a few minutes."

"Mr. Pokey?" Dan said with a groan.

Amy grinned. "At least you're not Shirley anymore."

As they rounded a corner, Jake Rosenbloom waved to her, holding open the door of a white taxi. In moments all four were zooming up the street toward one of Samarkand's most famous sites, Ulugh Beg Observatory.

Looking out the window, Amy saw a flat desert city ringed by mountains. The architecture was boxy and colorless, punctuated by the pale gold of minarets. It was as if all the creative energy had been spent in ancient times. She squinted, imagining a plain with tents, a wide avenue rutted from horses and oxen.

"Okay, Amy and I did research, and here's what we know," Atticus said. "From the fourth to the fourteenth century—Samarkand, whoa. *The* place. Center of the

Middle East, which is the center of the world. A Muslim coolness millennium!"

"The fifteenth, really," Amy corrected him. "So eleven hundred years."

"Uh, right, if you're being picky," Atticus went on. "So the Silk Road busts through here, everybody tooling around to trade stuff. Silk, food, jewelry . . . they're like, 'Beep beep, here come Indians! Russians! Chinese, Mongols, and Burmese!' Well, probably not 'beep beep,' but more like camels grunting and spitting—"

"Persians, too," Amy interjected. "From Mesopotamia. They were a huge part of this."

"Will you let him talk?" Dan demanded. *"He's* interesting."

Atticus pointed to a distant hill. "Picture this monster building over there. Traders on their yaks, talking away—'Forsooth, Mohammed, wazzat?' 'Lo, Vladimir, it's our observatory! Why, it's the envy of the world!' Only I guess in actuality they spoke different languages—"

"Wait. Who are Mohammed and Vladimir?" Dan said.

"I'm just painting a picture!" Atticus said.

"Maybe we should let Amy speak," Jake suggested. "Not that she's smarter, of course. Just quicker."

"Thanks, Jake." Even though his compliments were insults, she felt blood rush to her cheeks. "Samarkand was the capital city of a khanate—sort of like a country. Its leader's name was Taragai, but he was called

Ulugh Beg, which means 'Great Ruler.' He was also a genius—both a mathematician and astronomer. His school is still standing, and his observatory was the greatest in history."

"Hello?" Dan said, raising his hand in the backseat. "Before I drift off? I'm thinking, we're looking for some kind of orb, right? And that's what Ulugh Beg measured—orbs. Planets, stars, the moon?"

"Yes! Dan is right!" Atticus said. "So, Beg is obsessed with this stuff. He wants to plot the movements of celestial bodies. He wants to count all the stars in the sky—which only this Greek guy named Ptolemy had ever tried. But Beg is like, 'Hark, my sextants and handheld astrolabes are the ultimate in coolness, but not precise! Thus, I must rock the astronomical world!' So he builds this observatory—"

"Whoa, pause button, please," Dan said. "You're missing my point. The 'Medusa' led us to Rome, where we found the Marco Polo manuscript. It had the map, and the map led here. So far, everything has been about maps and locations. Astrid's list, McIntyre's list—*places*. Now we have to find . . . a stale orb? What does an orb have to do with locations—unless the location is, like, outer space?"

"I say we go in with an open mind," Amy said. "Beg made this Olympic-sized sextant—built right into the rock of the earth. The light came in through a hole in the roof. An enormous pendulum hung over these huge, semicircular stone tracks running due north-south. Astronomers would line up the stars and then record their positions on a curved wall. Over time they'd trace out paths, orbitals. Kind of like a planetarium, only upside down. The famous Fakhri sextant."

"I thought Famous Fakhri was a falafel place," Dan said.

"It's like this hundred-eighteen-foot roller-coaster track," Atticus said. "Made out of polished stone."

Dan's face lit up. "Sweet. Are we there yet?"

"Deep within Gurkhani Zij
Lies Taragai's unfinished prize:
The unperfected instrument,
Though vast in power, small in size!"

The tour guide, Salim Umarov, had a deep and dramatic voice. The hot wind blew his salt-and-pepper beard as he walked across a circular plateau, high over Samarkand. At the poem's last word, he paused and took a small bow under a crooked, stunted desert tree. In the distance behind him, the dappled stones of a cemetery stretched out below to the horizon. With his embroidered vest and loose, flowing white garments, he looked to Atticus like an ancient sage.

"This anonymous poem," he said, "is a recent archaeological find, procured for our library. Some think Ulugh Beg wrote it. But *Taragai* is actually his real name, so I do not think so."

Atticus felt his eyes closing. He'd barely slept the night before. He hadn't wanted to do all the research, but Amy was going strong, so he wanted to match her. Now he regretted it.

A flash of gold caught his eye and suddenly he was wide awake.

A familiar head of blond hair hovered above the heads of the crowd, coming closer to him.

Casper.

Backing slowly away from the crowd, Atticus tried to catch Dan's attention—Jake's, Amy's—but they were all rapt as the guide continued his speech.

How did he find me?

Why weren't the others noticing him? He was almost on top of them! Atticus opened his mouth to warn them, but no words came out.

"Young man! Be careful of the plinth!" Umarov called out.

Atticus's calf caught against a low wall. He hurtled backward to the ground. Jake was running toward him. The crowd was opening up. Casper was raising something in his hand—something that glinted in the sun. . . .

"Watch it, Jake!" Atticus shouted.

His brother lifted him to his feet. "'Sup, Att? Are you feeling all right?"

Behind him, the man with blond hair snapped a photo. He lowered the camera, revealed a bone-thin, grandfatherly face.

"I thought . . . that was Casper. . . ." Atticus said.

Jake turned. "We need to get you new glasses."

Dan was dusting off the back of Atticus's pantlegs now, and he picked up some coins that had fallen from Atticus's pocket. "Hey, I know how it feels. When really bad stuff happens, it's hard to shake it off."

"If Casper even thinks of coming within five miles, he's toast," Jake said. "We've all got your back, Att. Well, I do, at least."

"We do, too," Amy snapped.

Atticus nodded. He headed back to the group with Dan, taking deep, cleansing breaths.

"Plinth?" Dan said. "Is that like *plinth and needlth*?"

Atticus smiled. "It means the original foundations. That's what those low walls are. The library and stuff, they're all new — including that big fancy door, which leads to the Fakhri sextant."

Umarov led the group toward the door, walking between two low, calf-high walls that traced rectangles. "Imagine this empty plateau in the fourteen hundreds, well outside the firelight of Samarkand. So much pure darkness, bright stars! Ulugh Beg cataloged one thousand eighteen of them. Well, some scholars say one thousand twenty-two . . . but who's counting?"

The guide pulled the door open. Atticus and Dan raced to the front of the group to get in first. The temperature immediately dropped inside the door, as if the cold of outer space itself had been trapped over the centuries. A narrow stone path led to a wide railing overlooking a deep black hole.

Atticus's breath caught in his throat, and it wasn't because of the temperature. He had seen plenty of photographs of the Fakhri sextant, but they didn't do justice to the massive sweep of the stone slopes. They plunged into the earth like giant mammoth tusks, with matching stone stairs on either side. He wondered how slabs of such weight and size had been shaped so precisely, polished to a perfect circular curve. He imagined hundreds of slaves hammering through rock, carving stone in the arid heat, using specifications of the tiniest fraction of a circle — using *pi*! Then somehow they had to carry the slabs up a curved slope. And if it was just a centimeter off, the whole thing fell apart. "Whoa . . ." he said.

"Dude, you could make serious bank with a skateboard rental!" Dan said.

Amy, who had positioned herself near Dan, jabbed him in the side.

Umarov cocked his head, bemused. "A gnarly idea, indeed, as they say. Especially as the Fakhri sextant rose much, much higher." He gestured from the floor way upward behind them. "It curved up past where we are standing . . . into a building with a large dome."

Dan craned his neck upward. "Cool."

"It traces the north-south meridian exactly," Umarov said. "Ulugh Beg's measurements of stars and planets were accurate to one six-hundredth of a degree. This would be the width of an American penny at a distance of a third of a mile."

Atticus gazed at the battered, rough walls. Any kind of writing they could have read was gone.

"So that was it?" Dan said. "They hung out and waited for stars to move?"

Umarov struck another pose and recited:

"What of this work of Ulugh Beg,
Who dared to count infinity?
His catalog, though vast in scope,
Yet of divisions, had but three.

When listed in descending rank,
The Fakhri apex as a start,
Descend and rise, descend again,
And stand thee o'er my ruler's heart."

"What the heck does that mean?" Dan asked.

Umarov shrugged. "Theories abound. It may have been a key to how he worked. The sextant was indeed Ulugh Beg's heart. The pendulum descended and rose. The astronomer would stand at the bottom and look up along the shaft, visually lining up the star positions. The bodies were observed each day over many years, and each position was marked. Of course, stars orbit on many planes, so the formulae were complicated. So the 'divisions' could be the original buildings of the observatory. 'Descending rank' could be the position of the star as the light descends the pendulum. Or a reference to Beg's many smaller instruments, such as parallactic lineals, armillary spheres, handheld astrolabes—"

"Astro who?" Dan said.

"An astrolabe is a small version of a sextant," Umarov said. "Not as accurate, of course, but of great importance in early astronomy, for its portability. Many were exquisitely crafted, a perfect marriage of science and art."

Atticus peered down the length of the curve. What could Vesper One want—the enormous, heavy tracks themselves? "Excuse me," he said, "but if I said anything about a stale orb, would you know what I was talking about?"

The guide paused. He turned to Atticus with a smile and nodded amiably. "Why, yes, of course I do."

Four pairs of eyes snapped to the old man's face. "You do?" Amy cried out.

Bewildered, Atticus said, "Can you tell us how to find it?"

Umarov laughed as he reached into a pocket of his long, flowing robe. "Indeed I can. But if you call her *it*, I'm afraid she will kick you out."

He handed Atticus a card:

Antiques ✿ Exotica ☽ Fortunes Told

Estelle Urb

137 Kuk-Saray Street

CHAPTER 18

Estelle Urb . . . a stale orb.

Brilliant, Atticus thought, as the taxi raced past the graveyard into town. Not a mathematical hint, not a strange word game, but a homonym!

"This doesn't seem right," Jake said. "I think it's a mistake. A coincidence."

"In this life," Amy said, "there are very few coincidences."

Jake scoffed. "Thank you, World-Weary Winifred."

The driver was arguing on his cell phone, swerving wildly. He screeched to a stop in front of a small building with curtained windows. "My boss call," he said. "Someone call him looking for two American kids. So he want to know your names. I tell him I have *four* kids, and I hang up."

Jake murmured, "This means, 'I covered for you, so give me a big tip.'"

Atticus leaped out of the cab as Amy paid up. "Come along, Arthur . . . Julius . . . Leonard!"

Dan nearly fell out of the taxi, laughing. *"What?"*

Atticus waited until Amy and Jake were out. "It's the real names of the Marx Brothers," Atticus said. "To disguise our own names. Because maybe it was Interpol who called him!"

"It was a good instinct," Amy replied.

"I agree, Julius," Dan said.

Jake walked toward the door of number 137. "You're all crazy."

He knocked loudly. It was a dingy, neglected storefront nestled between two newer office buildings. The bell hung from a rusty electrical wire, and a faded, hand-drawn sign drooped low over the front door.

Atticus heard shuffling footsteps. The door pulled open an inch, and a pair of bloodshot eyes peered out. "Who is calling?" a woman's voice asked.

"Are you Estelle Urb?" Jake asked.

The face retreated, the chain slid back, and the door opened.

Stale, musty air wafted out. Cautiously Atticus stepped into a small, dark room. As his eyes adjusted, he saw fringed lamps, lopsided chests of drawers, faded rugs, and ticking wooden clocks. A thick layer of dust had settled over everything.

"Shop is upstairs," she growled, heading toward a rickety staircase. "You come. But do not wake Ruhan."

Atticus assessed her accent. *Latvian or Finnish. Maybe Estonian.* He followed Amy and Jake up the steps, turning to look for Dan.

But Dan was standing in the middle of the living

room, wheezing, his face pale. "Can't breathe. . . . asthma . . ."

Amy spun around. "He can't stay in here!"

"I'll get him outside," Atticus said, leaping to the floor. "You stay. Don't leave my brother alone."

He rushed Dan through the door and onto the sidewalk. Gasping, Dan pulled an inhaler out of his pocket and took two puffs. "Sorry," he said. "It hardly ever happens anymore. I need to walk."

Atticus took him by the arm and headed down Kuk-Saray Street. Sheltered by the buildings, the air still had a hint of morning coolness. Atticus loved the desert dryness in Samarkand. It seemed to sharpen each scent, so that a trip down a street was like a journey through forests of sweet juniper and cinnamon.

Now, as he breathed with Dan, he caught a whiff of something familiar.

Plov.

Years ago, Atticus had traveled with his dad to Tashkent and watched men filling a huge cauldron with layers of mutton, yellow carrots, currants, spices, and rice. They worked with amazing speed, their faces still and solemn—then they let it cook for hours in a pit, buried under thick blankets. *Plov* tasted so good, it nearly made him . . .

"Cry," Dan said.

"What?" Atticus replied, snapping out of his fantasy.

"I think I'm going to cry if I don't eat whatever that is," Dan answered.

Atticus nodded. "But it's dangerous to split up."

"Dangerous," Dan said dubiously.

"Unless we . . . " Atticus said.

Dan nodded. "Grab something quick."

Together they raced down the block. People were already leaving offices for lunchtime. The street was crowded with women in long, patterned dresses and bright-colored head kerchiefs. Many men wore small black-and-white-patterned skullcaps sewn with four seams at the side, so that the top formed a square.

At the end of the block, a set of stone steps led to a small market area lined with shops. In a food stand, a burly, mustached man stood over two simmering pots. They were small versions of the cauldron Atticus had once seen. He knew the smell. His mouth was already watering. "Is that *plov*?" Atticus asked.

The man nodded proudly. "Also *nochas*. Sweet yellow peas. Delicious."

"It's like that song," Dan murmured. "All you need is *plov* . . ."

Atticus grinned. "*Plov* makes the world go around . . ."

"I'm just a *plov* machine—"

"Also we have *non* bread," the man went on. He gestured toward a deep oven, where puffy breads were plastered to the inner walls, as if they'd grown there. "And *katyk* to drink. Made with yogurt and watermelon. Very nice."

Dan was looking over his shoulder, across the plaza.

"Order two of everything," he said, shoving cash into Atticus's hand. "I'll be right back. I need to get a souvenir."

"*Souvenir?*" Atticus said. "Wait. Shouldn't we stay together? I mean, people are after both of us!"

"No one knows who we are," Dan said. "I'm just going, like, twenty yards away. For a second. We'll be able to see each other. Don't worry."

He scampered toward a fabric shop just across the plaza. Before ducking inside, he gave a reassuring wave.

Atticus brought the food to a café table. He broke open some *non* bread, inhaling the yeasty warmth. He spooned some *plov* on top and folded it into a bite-sized hunk. As he raised it to his mouth, he spotted a figure sitting on a stool across the street.

Where'd he come from?

A moment ago, he hadn't been there. He was enormous and sweaty, the buttons of his white shirt straining against his expansive belly. He held a guitar but he was not yet playing. When Atticus looked up, he quickly turned away.

Atticus took a deep breath. It was easy to get paranoid. He needed to calm down. He took a bite and washed it down with *katyk*.

When he put the drink down, the wide-girthed guitarist had slid his stool closer.

Atticus's gaze darted across to the fabric shop. Dan had disappeared inside. The crowd was thickening now, and Atticus could barely see the door. He took another few bites and then stood.

As he moved across the plaza toward where Dan had gone, the man quickly got up. Placing his guitar on his stool, he headed for the shop. With a much smaller distance to cover.

"Dan!" Atticus shouted.

His voice was absorbed by the noisy throng. He pivoted, running back in the direction they'd come, weaving through the crowd, pushing people aside. A bearded old man shook his fist, yelling something in Uzbek.

He took the stairs two at a time. There were fewer people at the top. It was a clear shot back to Estelle Urb. He leaped to the top and began to run.

To his left, a man on a bike pedaled out of an alleyway. He skidded to a stop in front of Atticus.

"Hey, watch it!" Atticus shouted, veering to the right. The guy swerved, matching his motion.

Atticus stumbled, falling to one knee. He rose, panicked, glancing over his shoulder.

A beefy arm clasped his shoulder and spun him around. Atticus was face-to-face with the guitarist. The man was breathing heavily, his face red with exertion.

"Greetings, Atticus Rosenbloom," he said with a thick Uzbek accent.

CHAPTER 19

"It is the dried pupa of moth," said the old man behind the silk shop's counter, holding out a plate of shining giant insect shells. "Delicious."

"Uh, thanks," Dan said, holding back a wave of nausea, "but my true *plov* awaits outside."

"Eh?" the man replied.

"Never mind. Bad joke. I was wondering about something. These moths — they make the silk you sell, right? Are they *Bombyx mori* moths?"

The man looked impressed. "Ah, a serious young man! Yes, indeed, on both questions. We grow the *Bombyx mori* carefully. Use their cocoons for the silk. The shell for food. We are . . . how you say . . . a green business!"

Dan could barely contain himself. *The secretion of the* Bombyx mori *silk moth.* Of all the thirty-nine Clues, this was the hardest one to find.

What better place to find it than on the Silk Road?

"I was wondering," Dan said. "How much do you charge for the secretions?"

The man looked confused. "Secretions? You mean,

silk liquid—not silk itself? We can do this for you. Perhaps give it to you in a tube. But it must not be exposed to the air—"

Dan slapped a wad of cash on the counter. "I need what you've got, please."

The man's confused expression suddenly cleared. "Right away."

Moments later, Dan was walking out the door with a small tube of thick, white fluid. And his sixteenth ingredient. "Hey, Att!" he cried out. "Did you save me any—?"

Dan stopped at the table, where three middle-aged men were working their BlackBerrys. His and Atticus's meals were piled neatly on an empty seat.

"Did you see the kid who was just here?" Dan asked.

One man shrugged, one grunted, the other yelled at his screen.

"Atticus!" Dan turned around, scanning the crowd. At the top of the stairs, where they'd just come from, he saw a commotion. A large body. Flying dreadlocks.

He ran as hard as he could. Atticus was struggling with a guy on a bicycle and a human moose.

Dan powered up the steps, aiming his shoulders for the big man's knees. The guy teetered and dropped forward like a redwood. He grabbed on to Atticus.

All three of them fell to the street.

A small crowd had gathered around, staring in confusion. The large man sat up, placing one hand on Atticus's shoulder and the other on Dan's. "I did not know," he said, "it would be this hard to deliver message from Mark Rosenbloom. Atticus, your father asked me to tell you. Go home. He is very angry."

The sound of footsteps worked its way into Nellie's dream.

In it, she had set out a lavish buffet in her fantasy restaurant, Gomeztibles. But now dirt-encrusted jackboots were squashing her puff pastry. They were kicking veal scaloppine onto the wall, squirting blood from the blood pudding. . . .

"No!" she cried out.

The loud rap from the outside made her scream. She awoke into the familiar fetid air of the prison.

Curled against the wall, Natalie murmured in her sleep, "Kenilworth, will you be a dear and open the door?"

"Nat? Guys?" Nellie said. "They're here."

The entrance slid open. It hit the inner wall with a loud *whack*, raining dust onto the floor.

Three men in white suits stepped in. Each was wearing a black mask and had a holstered gun. One of them threw a pile of clean uniforms on the floor. Another shoved a large sheet of cardboard at Alistair, along with a small handwritten note. The old man read it. He looked bewildered. "You want me to copy these words onto this sheet? Whatever for?"

The man lifted his foot and drew it back to kick. Alistair flinched.

"Leave him alone!" Nellie shouted. "Al, just do it. Everyone, change into the uniforms. No questions. Now."

When they were changed, the men gestured for them to line up by the wall.

"Dear heavens," Fiske murmured, "if they're going to shoot us, what is the point of the clean clothing?"

"Shows off the blood better," Nellie drawled.

"That is not funny!" Natalie said, shaking violently as she backed against the wall.

Still doubled over from his injury, Phoenix led Ted to the wall. Ted put his arm around Natalie and stared defiantly ahead. Reagan stood next to him, arms folded. Nellie knelt in front, next to Alistair, who was still writing something on the cardboard. Fiske stood behind them, one comforting hand on each of their shoulders.

Nellie spotted a lizard skittering in through the open door. It was heading along the wall, behind the group. She was hoping Natalie the Squeamish wouldn't notice it.

No such luck.

"Eeeeee!" Natalie's screech was earsplitting. "That *thing* touched me! I'm poisoned! Get me a specialist!"

Nellie turned. The lizard was crouched by the wall, looking scared. It was beautiful, its complex black-and-white skin pattern like a mysterious, pixelated photograph. She reached over and picked it up. Its heart was beating a mile a minute. "You're scaring it,

Nat," she remarked. "Whoa. Easy, boy. Girl. Whatever."

It seemed to calm down in her hand. Nellie smiled. If she was going to die, her last act would be to give comfort to another living thing.

A metallic sound echoed sharply. Nellie set her jaw and looked up.

One of the guards was holding up a cell phone camera. "Say cheese," he said.

"What the—?" Reagan sputtered.

"Is this some sort of joke?" Fiske demanded.

"I don't think so," Alistair replied, lifting the cardboard sheet.

Nellie's pulse quickened. A digital photo. Which meant someone was going to see it. Which meant a possible connection to the outer world.

Make it count.

With a sudden, crazy idea, she raised the reptile toward the camera.

And she smiled.

"Cheese."

CHAPTER 20

They looked terrible.

Staring at the image of the hostages on her phone, Amy could barely hold back tears. Vesper One had sent it just as they'd walked back into their hotel room.

On the laptop screen, Sinead and Evan huddled around the image, which Dan had patched through to Sinead's phone.

"Wow," said Sinead on Dan's laptop. "They sure look . . ."

"Battered," Jake said.

"Desperate," Atticus added.

"Alive," Dan interjected.

All seven hostages were accounted for. That was the good part. The bad part was everything else. They stood against a flaking hole in the wall. Phoenix Wizard had a bloody gash on his forehead. Reagan Holt's wrist was bandaged and Natalie looked shrunken. Nellie seemed half-crazed, thrusting forward a lizard as if it were a sword.

But what had scared Amy the most was the sight of

Uncle Alistair. He was glaring at the camera, defiant. He clutched a handmade sign:

"That handwriting is familiar," Amy said.

On the screen, Evan nodded. "It's Alistair's. Vesper One made him draw his own sign. I'm figuring he didn't want anyone in the Vesper organization to do it. That would give us a handwriting sample to analyze. Pretty shrewd."

"Pretty paranoid," Dan said.

"Props to Dan for his quick thinking," Sinead said. "He forced Vesper One to take the photo. It may not look it, but the tide is turning, guys. Hostages alive, Atticus outwitting the Wyomings in Göreme—and we just heard from Jonah and Hamilton. They've arrived in Pompeii. Any progress on the stale orb?"

"It's not Estelle Urb," Jake said bitterly, touching a bandaged arm. "That was a wild-goose chase—just like I predicted."

"What happened to your arm?" Sinead asked. "It looks all scratched up."

"The old lady told us 'Do not wake Ruhan,'" Jake replied, "but who knew Ruhan was a chimpanzee? Apparently I said something that sounded like 'I ate your bananas' in Estonian. Then I was rewarded for my pains by learning that Atticus had gone rogue."

"In actuality, Dan and I were just getting some *plov*," Atticus said, "but Dad had been trying to track us by calling cab companies. It must have been the call our driver took—and the guy ratted us out. So Dad contacted an old student who'd moved here to get a PhD. He was also making some money as a musician—and he found me. Oh, by the way, Jake, Dad wants us home."

"I'll talk to him," Jake said.

Amy was zoning out of the conversation. She stared at the image of the hostages. A pair of eyes seemed to be reaching out at her.

Nellie's.

The au pair seemed manic. Borderline deranged.

I know that expression.

It was exactly the way Nellie looked when she would thrust out her iPod. *Amy, you just HAVE to listen to this!*

"What's with the lizard?" Atticus asked, looking

over her shoulder. "That girl looks possessed."

"Maybe she was bitten," Jake chimed in. "Reptile venom can cause hallucinations. Which you would know if you had watched the recent *National Geographic* special on South Africa."

Amy's breath caught.

She's not asking us to listen. She's asking us to see.

"Do you *know* that the lizard is South African, Jake?" Amy asked.

"I was being illustrative," Jake said. "I don't really know where it comes from."

Amy grinned.

Nellie's not crazy. She's the only one in this photo who's still thinking.

"Jake, thank you!" she exclaimed, grabbing him by the shoulders and planting a kiss on his cheek.

Jake's eyes widened. He touched the side of his face. "Wore yelcome. I mean—"

On the screen, Evan's jaw hung open in shock. "Amy?"

"Evan, Sinead—look at Nellie in that photo!" Amy said. "She's trying to tell us something. What do we know about that lizard? The size, the pattern of its skin—they'll indicate what part of the world it's from. We'll know where the hostages are being held!"

"Sister, you are the best!" Sinead exclaimed. "We'll get to work on it, stat."

Amy smiled. *Sister.* She liked the sound of that. Sinead's expression warmed her. It was the only glimmer of happiness she'd had all day.

"Um, Ames?" Evan said, his voice a little unsteady. "That was brilliant. Really. I, uh, I just wanted to weigh in on how . . . brilliant you are. 'Cause, yeah. I've been thinking about that. And, um, you."

"Thanks, Evan," Amy said. "And Sinead. Oh, and thank Ian, too!"

Sinead and Evan shot each other a glance. Their smiles vanished.

"Um, that was the other thing we need to tell you," Sinead said softly. "Ian is gone. He left a note saying he was going to New York. He didn't say why, but we know Isabel is there."

"Isabel?" The name was like a sharp slap. Amy's exhilaration drained instantly. "But why?"

"We don't know, and his phone is not working," Sinead said. "I'd like to say he misses his mom. But I don't think Isabel is missable."

"He should have contacted us by now," Evan said.

"Do you think he's been kidnapped?"

"Don't know." Sinead shrugged sadly. "We'll find out."

Amy exhaled hard.

Don't think about Ian.

There had to be an explanation for his absence. Ian had changed. He'd proven that. Attleboro would take care of this misunderstanding. Right now there were way more important things on hand.

Uncle Alistair's words seemed to jump out of the

image—*One and a half days left*. It wasn't much time to solve a mystery locked up for six hundred years. And she had only a thin pile of papers from an egghead museum guide to unlock it.

Or they would all have blood on their hands.

"Gooooood afternoon, this is meteorologist Sandy 'the Breeze' Bancroft, with *Disaster Watch!* We're reporting live from the ultimate death-doom-and-destruction destination—that's right . . . Pompeii!"

With a frown of deep concern, a bronze-faced weather forecaster gestured to Mount Vesuvius behind him. His hair flew straight backward, courtesy of a gigantic offscreen fan.

Hamilton Holt stopped and turned to look, stepping on Jonah Wizard's shoes. "Whoa—it's the Breeze! The Disaster Forecaster, the Sultan of Storms! I can't believe this!"

"I can't believe you just scuffed my custom four-hundred-fifty-dollar Nikes," Jonah said. But already Hamilton was charging the set, like a running back on fourth and goal.

Erasmus checked his watch. "The museum will close soon. We'll be late."

"We gotta extract Ham from Mr. Tan-from-a-Can." Jonah pulled his hood tight to obscure the Face That Launched a Million Downloads. "Keep with me, be cool, go with the flow. Anyone asks, my name is

Clarence, yo. I just happen to resemble the international artist Jonah Wizard. Got that?"

Erasmus nodded. "Clarence Yo."

"What kind of crew *are* you guys?" Jonah muttered, heading into the crowd.

Bancroft dropped his head portentously at the camera. "We'll be back after a commercial break, with more—"

"Daily doom in your living room!" Hamilton recited aloud.

The camera light went out, and Bancroft narrowed his eyes at Hamilton. "An American fan. Sweet! Hey, fella, how'd you like a coupon for one dollar off a box of Sandy's Volcano-Hot Bancroft Breezcuits?"

As Jonah pushed through the crowd, he felt the love all around. Crowds were like oxygen to him. Only a thin piece of fabric separated his peeps from the *gangsta di tutti gangstas*. He could remove the hood and give them what they hungered for. The face.

But he wasn't going to do that. He was all about the plan. And the plan was Pompeii. Getting the 411 on Astrid Rosenbloom's list. Rescuing Phoenix.

But first, the extraction of Hamilton.

The Breeze was signing Ham's coupon. "Write 'To my biggest—and I mean biggest—fan,'" Hamilton said.

Jonah pulled on his arm. "Yo, Human Action Figure. We gotta keep the focus."

Sandy Bancroft looked up. "Why does that sound familiar?"

I gotta stop dropping lyrics from real songs! Jonah scolded himself. "Uh, just sayin'."

Bancroft cocked his head. " 'Just Sayin' — my kids *love* that song!"

Jonah cringed at his own carelessness. "Yo, *you* talk to him, Erasmus," he whispered over his shoulder.

Erasmus yanked Hamilton by the arm. "Got to run. Thanks, Mr. Breeze."

As they turned to go, Jonah nearly rammed into a girl wearing an I WENT TO POMPEII AND MET THE LAVA MY LIFE T-shirt. "Yo, don't touch the merch," he said.

The girl's jaw dropped open.

Oops.

"Let's roll!" Jonah shouted, breaking into a sprint. "We got about three seconds! Where to?"

"The Antiquarium!" Erasmus said, struggling to keep pace. "Pompeii's museum. The biggest resource about the explosion. *Why are we running?*"

"Just do it!" Jonah said.

Clutching his coupon, Hamilton grinned. "You have no idea how much this means to me."

"It's about to mean a whole lot more!" said Jonah, as a gust of wind blew the hood off his face.

A bloodcurdling shriek rang out behind him. "*JO-O-O-O-NAH!*"

Jonah could feel the pavement shaking under his feet.

He wasn't sure if it was the mob or the volcano.

CHAPTER 21

Sometimes, Ian Kabra thought, it paid to be devastatingly handsome.

With a big smile, he strode up to the United Nations security guard. She looked exactly like her photo in the Cahill database.

Reina Mendez. Age 37. 144-36 Steinway Place, Astoria. Daughter, Pilar. Fifth grade, PS 151Q, gifted in math and chemistry, scheduled for accelerated math on New York State standardized test.

"Good morning, Reina," he said, holding out his fake ID to the guard. He had created it in a hurry and the resolution was off. "How did your daughter's math exam go?"

The guard looked momentarily bewildered.

Ian boosted his smile to level five: irresistible. Reina glanced briefly at the faked ID card. "Ninety-seven out of a hundred," she said with pride. "Thank you for asking, Mr. . . . um, Kabra."

"Bravo, a budding genius," Ian said. "Education

begins in the home, I always say. As does personal attractiveness."

"You should know, sir," the guard replied.

I know more than you imagine, Ian thought as he breezed into the main lobby. Access to the Cahill database had its advantages. Like private surveillance records of every UN employee. Ian could have told Reina the date of her appendix operation, every item in her last grocery purchase, and the fact that she had a medical history of intense foot odor.

But achieving entry into the building was enough.

He rode to the second floor. From there, the crowd noise guided him. It was an unmistakable din of excitement, an electricity he could feel even before leaving the elevator. To his right, a throng spilled out the door of a vast auditorium. People of all ages and nationalities jockeyed for position, straining to see the lecture inside.

"Pardon me . . . clear, please. . . ." Ian said, sliding through the crowd.

Although her face loomed overhead on two enormous screens, Ian almost didn't recognize his own mother.

It was the smile.

It dazzled. It beamed. It bathed the room in warmth. And it shocked Ian to the core. She had only rarely displayed that much brightness to her children. Usually after a successful poisoning or international art theft.

She was standing behind a lectern, center stage, before a bank of press microphones. Behind her, an image flashed onto another screen, drawing gasps and applause. Ian recognized it from the home page of the website of Mother's organization. The lush South American jungle outpost. A happy, banana-eating child surrounded by young workers of many ethnicities.

"Meet dear, precious Carlos," Isabel said, her voice sweet and melodious. "He weighed a mere thirty pounds when he came to our station in Sierra de Córdoba, Argentina. Dressed in rags, mewling softly. He appeared more animal than human. But look at him now! In a few short months, a thriving young man. A boy who can read Dr. Seuss in two languages and navigate the web. Whose final words before going to sleep at night are . . ."

Her voice faded away, and a video faded in — there was Carlos in pajamas, with a gap-toothed smile, holding Isabel's hand. ". . . THANK YOU, AY DOUBLE-U DOUBLE-U!" he shouted.

A woman sitting next to Ian burst into tears. The audience rose to its feet, exploding with applause. Someone began shouting "Ka-BRA . . . Ka-BRA!" and soon the entire audience had joined him.

"Please . . . please, no, the credit does not belong to me. . . ." Isabel shook her head modestly, as if embarrassed beyond her wildest dreams. "It is the work, not I. It is the mission of a hundred souls . . . to help a million!"

The few remaining sitters stood, pounding their

palms together. If the UN could adopt a resolution of sainthood, Isabel Kabra would be top of the list.

Ian jammed his hands in his pockets. He bit his tongue to keep from screaming.

As the presentation wound down, people lined the aisle to see Isabel. Several mothers had brought children. Almost everyone was carrying a copy of her recent book, *Listening to the Banana Leaf: Saving the World, One Soul at a Time.*

Ian took a place in line. He waited for what seemed like hours, and then there they were. Eye to eye for the first time since the gauntlet.

"Ian, darling," she said, "I was expecting you."

Ian sputtered. In his head, anger and shock and longing all collided, canceling one another out and leaving him nearly speechless. *"Expecting me?"*

"It was only a matter of time before you left those . . . people," Isabel said, avoiding the word *Cahills* as if pronouncing it would be like sipping a beaker of smallpox. "So, Ian, do you have a question? Or are you here to volunteer and do something useful with your life for a change?"

"I want to chat, Mother," Ian said with forced cheer. "About your vacation plans. Just an FYI, in case you were considering another jaunt to that delightful little backwater in upstate New York. You won't be able to tour the DeOssie factory anymore. Although the crater that remains is bound to attract a lively crowd."

"Ian, dear, you speak in riddles," Isabel replied.

"Riddle me this, Mother," Ian said. "What does Aid Works Wonders have to do with the Vespers?"

Ian watched her carefully. Mother was the master of the impassive expression. She often bragged that she had total control over each of her facial muscles. But he knew better than that. Even after not seeing her for two years, he could detect a tiny tightening of the left side of her lip.

Ian reached out and brushed his finger against his mother's forehead. "Odd — you're sweating, Mother. Yet the room is awfully well air-conditioned. Oh, by the way, your daughter is still alive for now, thanks for asking. Although she appears to be starving. Since you care so much about little Carlos, surely you want to know about your own blood —"

"Carlos *is* my blood," Isabel snapped, lowering her voice to a focused whisper. "When my children left me, my world ended. I was thrown in prison, no different from your sister. I learned there. I discovered the meaning of compassion for others. Giving of oneself. Loyalty."

"Loyalty to what, Mother?" Ian asked. "What *do* you believe in?"

Isabel cupped Ian's face gently in her hand. "Ask yourself that question, my handsome son. Why are you here? Why did you leave your new family?"

"I didn't leave them!" Ian retorted.

"Do *they* see that? Face it, Ian, they tolerate you, that's all. In their minds, you'll always be an outsider.

And now you're gone. *Snap*—there goes that fragile bond. Do you believe they'll let you back?" Isabel threw her head back in mocking laughter. "People trust me, Ian. Who trusts you?"

"I—I—" Ian stammered.

"Next, please?" Isabel was already gesturing to the person behind him.

Ian turned. He elbowed his way through the adoring mass. No one seemed to pay him the slightest attention.

Outside the auditorium, a table with Aid Works Wonders merchandise was six deep. People were buying buttons and bumper stickers for fifteen dollars. "Each purchase will feed an entire family for a month!" a worker chirped loudly, displaying a sticker that said: MAKE A FAMILY HAPPY—CHANGE THE WORLD!

An entire family.

The notion was staggering. Fifteen dollars was the dry-cleaning bill for Ian's hand-painted Italian silk tie. Since his fall from Kabra wealth, he knew the prices of things. For that to be the price of a family's happiness? Unimaginable. In fact, he couldn't imagine a happy family at all.

Waiting for the elevator, Ian gazed out the window. He watched an airliner swoop low overhead on its way to LaGuardia Airport. From here, the airport was a short cab ride away.

He contemplated texting Attleboro with an update. But he changed his mind.

You'll always be an outsider. . . .

Some things just had to be done solo.

Flipping open his phone, he navigated to his browser window, which showed a confirmation of his flight to Boston.

In the upper right corner, he clicked on a link: CHANGE FLIGHT DESTINATION.

"Maybe *stale orb* means something in Persian," Dan said as he brushed his teeth. "Some special saying from Ulugh Beg's time. Like that Greek dude shouting 'Eureka' when he invented souvlaki or whatever. You know, like . . . 'Look, Abdul. Star number one thousand! Woo-hoo! Stale orb!'"

"It was Archimedes," Amy replied, looking up from her pile of papers. "And he discovered the principle of buoyancy. Oh, and, Dan? Ulugh Beg influenced generations, right up to Tycho Brahe. He estimated the length of a year and the angle of the earth's tilt to unbelievable accuracy. But he didn't say 'Woo-hoo! Stale orb!'"

"Okay, okay, just trying to think outside the planetarium," Dan said, spitting in the sink. "You know, chop open the mystery with my mental parall . . . ax? Get it?"

"If I read one more word about parallaxes, celestial declinations, astrolabes, sextants, quadrants, and gnomons," Amy said, rubbing her eyes, "I'll scream."

It was nearly two-thirty A.M. and she had pored over every word of Umarov's material at least twice. There was no doubt about Ulugh Beg's awesomeness. But awesomeness had its limits. For one thing, it wasn't going to save Uncle Alistair.

"Wait," Dan said. "Did you say *parallaxes*? Is that the plural? I thought it was, you know, one parallack, two parallacks."

"There's no such thing as *a parallack*, Dan!" Amy replied. "Now either come out and help or go to sleep."

"Hey, sorry." Suddenly, Amy heard Dan's toothbrush clatter into the sink. "Hold on. You nailed it, big sister!"

"Nailed what?" Amy said.

"The word *a*," Dan said. "Vespy is not asking us to find stale orb — he's asking us to find *a* stale orb. What if the *a* is supposed to be in there? A, S, T, A, L, E, O, R, B."

"So?" Amy asked.

"Remember when I said this thing was an anagram?" Dan asked. "Maybe I wasn't wrong after all! Let's try it with the *a* added in."

Amy looked over Dan's shoulder as he began writing:

ROTE BALSA
A SLOB TEAR
SLATE BOAR
ARAB STOLE

Dan nearly leaped out of his chair. "That's it! *Arab stole!* It was something stolen by a famous Arab. You know the history. Was anyone jealous of Ulugh Beg? Would some other astronomer want to take something of his?"

"People were mad at him," Amy said. "His own son beheaded him. But that's because Ulugh Beg became cruel as he got older. He sometimes murdered his own subjects."

"Why?" Dan said. "Did any of them steal something important? Something that might still be hidden?"

But Dan's words were fading as she rearranged the letters of ARAB STOLE in her mind. "Hold it, Sherlock," she said, grabbing her pen back.

Carefully she wrote out one word:

ASTROLABE

CHAPTER 22

```
** ALERT **
Kabra, I. Canceled flight.
```

Sinead stared slack-jawed at the text message on her screen. So he'd gone to New York. And now he wasn't coming back.

This was the wrong time for a crisis.

She sent a quick message to Ian—

```
Where r u?
```

A moment later she received her answer, the same as last time:

```
Out of Network
```

With a deep sigh, she lowered her head into her hands.

I should have expected this.

She'd worked with Ian. Tolerated him. Given him

the benefit of the doubt. She always knew he had a lot of hidden qualities. The problem was, they were all bad ones.

"Mrrp?" said Saladin, who was sitting on the desk with an *I-told-you-so* look.

"There must be an explanation," Sinead said.

"Braachh!" Saladin coughed up a hair ball and slunk away, nose in the air.

It was twenty minutes to seven. Evan would be arriving any minute. Sinead couldn't afford to be sidetracked. By now she'd hoped to nail the problem at hand.

The identification of Nellie's lizard.

The photo had been blurry and pixelated. But Attleboro's state-of-the-art image-enhancing software could sharpen the blurriest blob into an accurate high-res depiction. Sinead had worked hard on the parameters so it would predict the type of lizard by comparing length, coloration, proportion, anatomy.

First, she needed to prep the image. On a magnification of eight hundred, she shifted a pixel here, a pixel there. To help things along. Then she pressed ENTER.

RENDERING . . .

Within a microsecond, the software produced three possibilities: lizards from New Zealand, North Africa, and Argentina.

She stared at them all carefully. Which one?

But before she could get to work, another message popped up. It was from an Ekaterina operative in the

Cambridge University zoology department.

```
Thanks for the JPG . . . Working on it
now — Agent BullCommando2
```

Sinead's fingers paused in midair. *I never sent any inquiries. . . .*

No one was supposed to know about this. Nellie's lizard was classified.

Instantly another message appeared. An Ekat in Kentucky.

```
Reached out to SwampHamster1 at the
Cincinnati zoo for reptile verification.
— SneakyRed1.
```

And another:

```
Was there a sound file with that,
ClueCommander1?
```

The door flew open and Evan rushed in. "Sorry I'm late," he said. "My mom grilled me because the faculty adviser for speech club told her I wasn't—"

"ClueCommander1—that's your code name, isn't it?" Sinead asked, pointing to the message on the screen. "You sent out the lizard image to the Cahill Command Message Board!"

"Yup, from my cell phone," Evan explained. "Don't

worry. It's encrypted to two thousand forty-eight bits. Even the CIA doesn't use that level."

Sinead couldn't believe her ears. This was what you got when you trusted an outsider. "Evan, you never got clearance to do that!"

"But it's just you and me here," Evan said. "I thought—"

"And Dan and Amy don't count—or Jonah, Erasmus, and Hamilton?" With a sigh, Sinead flopped back in her chair. "The Cahill Command Message Board has *thousands of people*, Evan. We can encrypt all we want, but we don't know some of them very well. What if some renegade Tomas goes after the hostages alone, trying to be a hero? What if a dozen different Cahills come up with a dozen different lizard identifications? What if there's a mole—a Vesper who reports this whole search back to the top? *You're supposed to clear message board use!*"

"Ouch." Evan sank into a chair. "Okay, so, um, wait . . . I'll send another message, taking it all back?"

Sinead shook her head wearily. "Too late, Evan."

Time for some serious changes.

Attleboro security was supposed to be state of the art, but in minutes, it had become a joke. This was not acceptable. She opened a file cabinet drawer and took out a small ankle bracelet. "Look, just for a week or so, I would like you to wear this under your socks."

"A GPS tracker?" Evan looked at her in disbelief. "You're kidding, right? You're treating me like a spy?"

"I plan to give one of these to Erasmus and Jonah and Hamilton when they get back," Sinead said.

"But not Ian?" Evan asked.

"Ian is gone," Sinead shot back. "He went to New York on a moment's notice, then canceled his flight back."

"But his mom is there!" Evan said. "Maybe it's her birthday and he wants to surprise her."

"And maybe it's snowing purple gumdrops," Sinead said. "His mom is Isabel Kabra, Evan! The woman who killed Amy and Dan's parents, who shot her own daughter! From now on, I need records of all of our movements. Not only for security, but for your own protection."

Evan stood abruptly, his face growing red. "I designed that bracelet, for use with enemies. I set up over two hundred safeguards for us. For weeks, I have been lying to my friends and family in order to come here. I spend every minute of every day thinking of ways to rescue the hostages and get Amy and Dan back home safe. I may not be a Cahill, but I'm the only one who knows how to do anything here."

"Evan, please," Sinead said.

"And I am not wearing a tracker bracelet," Evan said as he stormed out the door.

Vesper Four loathed privacy. It was for weak-minded saps. People with shaky self-esteem.

But when you were a Vesper, you did what you had to do.

The room was dark and quiet. Soon it would be necessary to return to the hubbub and excitement. To the world that suspected nothing.

What a dark week. The Turkish stronghold had blown up, Vesper Six had failed, phone security had been breached, Interpol was still on the case, the hostages tried to escape, and the boy got his photograph.

Vesper One would be angry. Heads would roll.

But what a stroke of luck today had brought! The big man was going to love the news.

Vesper Four smiled. The sounds were growing louder outside the door. In a moment, people would be knocking. This wouldn't take long.

```
V-1: Lucky break. Contact established
with the Cahills. Exactly where you'd
expect. Will track. Can kill. Awaiting
instructions.

—V4
```

CHAPTER 23

Evan Tolliver hunched over his phone. The duck pond in back of the school was deserted but the air was freezing. He had only a moment between the end of school and the beginning of Robotics Club.

"Evan?" came Amy's voice.

She sounded so close. He could barely speak for the grin on his face. And the cold. "Hey, Ames! Just checking in. How's it going?"

"It's late here," Amy said.

"I know. Sorry," Evan replied. "I just—wanted to hear your voice. You sound great."

"Yeah," Amy said. "Same here."

Evan frowned. He thought he could hear someone else in the room. "Is someone there?"

"Dan," Amy quickly replied. "It's our hotel room. And . . . the Rosenblooms."

"Oh," Evan said. "Um, well . . . Sinead and me . . . I mean, Sinead and I . . . we had kind of a fight. She wants me to wear a tracking device."

He could hear Amy sigh. "Oh, Evan. Look, just do

what she says, okay? Ian's not around, and she needs you there more than ever. We need you."

We need you. Evan loved the sound of that. "Okay, I'll do it," he said softly. "I promise. Good luck with tomorrow, Ames. I know you'll find what you need. But stay safe. Because I need you."

"I will," Amy said. "Bye, Evan."

"Bye."

He hung up and sat still for a long while, trying to feel positive. Trying not to obsess over the fact that he hadn't heard what he'd been hoping to hear:

I need you, too.

Jake tapped Amy's wrist gently. "Hey, your eyes are closing."

"No, they're not," Amy replied, shaking the sleepiness out of her brain. In the wee hours of the morning, only she and Jake were still up. Atticus had fallen asleep on the sofa. Dan had disappeared into the bathroom a half hour ago and most likely dozed off in there.

"They were," Jake said. "I was watching them."

Amy cocked her head. "You were watching my eyes?"

"Well, not *watching*," Jake said. "Checking. Just to make sure we were staying on track. That's all."

She wasn't totally sure, but she thought she could see his face turning red.

It made her feel a slight tickle inside, like the flutter

of moth wings. *Stop that!* Why was she even wasting a nanosecond teasing this guy? He was exactly the kind of guy she didn't like, a hottie who knew he was a hottie. Thereby canceling the hotness completely.

Well, not completely.

She took a deep breath. She needed to stay on track.

Astrolabe. They had the word. But they didn't know what to do with it. She tried to focus on Umarov's poem.

Deep within Gurkhani Zij
Lies Taragai's unfinished prize,
(The unperfected instrument:) Astrolabe?
Though vast in power, small in size.

What of this work of Ulugh Beg,
Who dared to count infinity?
His catalog, though vast in scope
Yet of divisions, had but three.

When listed in descending rank,
The Fakhri apex as a start,
Descend and rise, descend again,
And stand thee o'er my ruler's heart.

"Bet you can say it by heart," Jake asked. "Any progress on what it means?"

Amy turned the paper so he could see. "Well, we know 'Gurkhani Zij' is the observatory. And 'Taragai' is Ulugh Beg's real name."

Jake looked carefully. "So deep within the observatory lies his 'unfinished prize, / The unperfected instrument . . . vast in power . . . small in size.' I'm guessing that's the astrolabe?"

"Most likely," Amy replied. "It's a small instrument. But it's not very powerful."

"What if Ulugh Beg was trying to perfect some kind of supercharged astrolabe?" Jake said. "A portable, totally accurate instrument, six hundred years earlier than the ones we have today?"

Amy nodded. It made sense. "So, by studying the Fakhri sextant in its full size, he could learn how to miniaturize it. Right, Jake. A discovery like that would have been huge in the fourteen hundreds."

"The question is, why would Vesper One want it?" Jake asked. "It's just an astronomical thingie."

"Let's find the thingie first. After ten-fifty P.M. tomorrow, when Uncle Alistair is safe, we can ask why." Amy rubbed her eyes and pored over the poem again. "Okay, the 'Fakhri apex' is the top of the Fakhri sextant. Looks like we start there."

Jake leaned in to look. "'His catalog, though vast in scope' . . . What's his catalog?"

"The count he made of all the stars," Amy said. "One thousand eighteen of them."

"'Of divisions had but three' — so let's divide the

number of stars into three parts," Jake suggested.

Amy turned a sheet of mathematical scribbles she'd made. "I tried that. But the number doesn't have three factors. Only two."

$$1{,}018 = 2 \times 509$$

"Yo, Att, wake up, we need all hands on deck," Jake called out to his brother.

Atticus sprang up from the couch and stumbled over. He glanced at the notes and recoiled. "Math. Very dangerous. Let Dan go first."

"Dan?" Amy called out to the bathroom door.

A barely audible grunt responded.

"Should I break in and get him?" Atticus asked.

"No," Amy said. "He's been working hard today. Let him rest. And if he falls asleep and has a sore butt in the morning, at least he won't be trying to slide down the Fakhri sextant."

Inside the bathroom, Dan was wide awake. The butt in question was cushioned by a fluffy hotel towel, folded and placed on the closed toilet lid.

His eyes were glued to a message that had appeared on his phone screen ten minutes earlier:

```
Okay, I know I need to be patient. But
it's been a while, Dan. I'm thinking maybe
```

you're angry? Or confused? Oh, well. I've been patient and hopeful for a long time. I can hold out a few more hours or days.

Please understand that the endgame is coming closer. What you see isn't what it seems. What appears to be cruelty is kindness. What seems needless pain is mercy. Maybe none of this makes sense now, but it will very soon.

One last thing. You have to trust me if you value the future of the world. And the love between father and son.

AJT

A droplet of sweat fell from Dan's brow. It splatted on the screen, mottling the words.

My father's words.

Dan wiped off the moisture and looked at the message again. No mystery, no vague hints. AJT had said the things he'd only hinted at before.

Father and son. There it was, in black and white.

Since the fire, Dan had lived with a disease. It wasn't anything visible, but he felt something had burrowed into his soul. He had learned to live with loss. He had protected himself. All his life, he'd turned away from the sight of boys playing catch with their dads, holding hands to cross the street. He fought against the envy, told himself that some things were simply impossible.

Now, with three words, the impossible was a click away. An opportunity to climb a bridge into the past. Or into utter darkness.

Or more likely, both.

What's happening to me?

He had vowed to turn his back on the darkness. To set the bridge aflame. But now he sat there, thumbs frozen over the keypad. Again.

He had composed a response but deleted it, three times. It felt like writing to a ghost. What happened when the dead became alive again? What happened to feelings that had been beaten down over nine years?

How wide did a river have to be until it was too wide to cross?

Who was Arthur J. Trent, anyhow?

Cruelty is kindness . . . pain is mercy. . . .

A Vesper, no doubt. That question had been settled in Dan's mind now. Answering the message meant betraying the Cahills. Throwing aside the gauntlet and everything he believed in. Making a pact with the murderer of William McIntyre.

A sudden pounding on the bathroom door made him jump to his feet.

"Yo, what happened? Did you fall in?" came Jake's voice.

The door flew open, and Dan snapped the phone shut.

CHAPTER 24

Ian Kabra could not understand why people liked driving for themselves. It was needlessly complicated. It involved skill and attention. It made you sweat and caused your leg to cramp. It was an action best left to hired professionals. He was simply not cut out for maneuvering a rented Jeep in a godforsaken South American jungle that made upstate New York look like the Riviera.

But necessity, Ian had decided, was the mother of combustion.

"Turn right," chirped the voice on his GPS device. "Now."

"Now?" Ian barked back. "All I see is a bloody narrow gap between trees!"

"Recalculating," the voice replied.

Now Ian was detecting an attitude. *Are we due for an eye exam, or did we fall asleep at that turn? I do have better things to do than recalculate every few seconds for the rest of my life.*

"Blast it," Ian murmured, stepping on the brake.

A buzz like a chain saw sounded in his ear, and he slapped a mosquito the size of a small nesting bird. At the airport, they had warned him to slather bug repellent above the neck. But he'd ignored them, and now his face felt like a Janus dartboard in a Lucian recreation room.

Ian yanked the steering wheel and skidded into a U-turn, then backtracked to the turnoff. This time, he forced his way down the impossibly thin path. "I hope you're happy now," he muttered to the machine.

"Destination reached," the voice said.

Ian slammed on the brake again. "Destination? *Here?*"

He wanted to hurl the device clear to Venezuela. This couldn't possibly be the South American headquarters of Aid Works Wonders. He was at the edge of a clearing in the forest — desolate, empty, neglected.

Ian stepped out of the car, grabbing a camera off the seat — along with a photo printout from the Aid Works Wonders website. The remains of a fire smoldered in the center of the clearing. Stacked around the edge were several piles of wood and papers. A gray fox, warming itself by the fire, gave Ian a wary look and then loped away.

As he stepped farther in, Ian could see the tottering frame of a hut, oddly lopsided. A broken sign dangled from the top of a door frame. Half of it was on the ground, the remaining part hand-painted with the words AID WOR.

He held up the photo. It was the same building—the one with all the workers posed in front. But in the image, it looked strong and substantial, not slanted like this.

Walking around the side, Ian saw why. It was only the frame of a building—a wall, a door. The rest had been propped up with rebar.

The other huts in the clearing had long since fallen down, swept into the piles along the edge. Ian edged close to one of the piles. It contained a stack of papers, including the corner of a glossy photo. He slid it out carefully.

The image of a young face smiled up at him—gap-toothed and impossibly cute. Two lines of text were stamped at the bottom: ROBERT J. RODRIGUEZ / REPRESENTED BY FILMKIDS TALENT AGENCY. But Ian knew the boy as someone else.

"Carlos," he murmured.

A gunshot rang out behind him. Ian screamed, falling to the ground.

"*¿Quién es?*" a voice bellowed. Three men came into the clearing. They were middle-aged and pot-bellied, wearing old shirts and straw hats. The man in the middle carried a pistol. Seeing Ian's face, he smiled. "*Americano?*"

Ian scrambled to his feet. "No, British! Look what you did to my trousers. These were custom tailored at Harrods. My tailor, Cedric—"

He let the sentence go. In truth, he hadn't seen Cedric in months.

"If you prefer," said the man in the middle, pointing his gun at Ian's leg, "I can make the other side match."

"No!" Ian shrieked. "I didn't realize you spoke a form of English. I am Ian Kabra. *Ka . . . bra!* Does that name ring a bell?"

A flash of recognition passed across the leader's face. He muttered something in Spanish to one of the other men, then lowered his gun. "I am Marcos. The woman . . . Kabra . . . she is your mother?"

"*Sí. Oui.* However you say it. Yes." Ian nodded, holding out the photo. "I came looking for this compound."

The three men gazed at it briefly and broke into laughter. "Look, there I am," Marcos said, pointing to a face in the image. "Also Miguel. And José. And all of our families."

Ian gazed closely at the picture. All three men were in the crowd, dressed in AWW uniforms. "You don't work for the organization?" he asked.

Marcos scowled. "Your mother did not let us keep the clothing. She told us we were going to be in movies. But she left and we did not hear from her again."

Ian took a deep breath. "My mother," he said as he took the photo back, "lies."

CHAPTER 25

Amy hit the ground hard, just inside the observatory wall. The pain shot up her leg but she shook it off. In the darkness, she could hear Jake, Atticus, and Dan drop on either side of her.

She listened for the shriek of a security system. Nothing. "Good job, Dan," she said.

"Thank my security guru, Lightfinger Larry," Dan said.

Her watch now read 9:47. The hike through the cemetery that bordered the observatory seemed to have taken hours, but Amy had decided going by foot was the only way to avoid detection. "We have exactly one hour and three minutes," she whispered.

She darted up the hill, hopping over the observatory plinth. The door to the Fakhri sextant loomed overhead, silhouetted by a thick canopy of stars.

"Do you think Ulugh Beg will forgive us for breaking in?" Atticus asked.

"We'll make him an honorary Cahill," Amy said.

"Stand back, guys." Jake spun sharply, lashing his

leg out in a powerful kick. He connected with the door, just above the latch.

It cracked open.

"Where'd you learn to do that?" Dan asked.

"Thank my martial-arts guru, Heavyfoot Harry," Jake replied.

"Come on." Amy pushed the door open and stepped inside. Jake shone a flashlight around the tunnel, focusing down the long slope of the sextant.

The air was frigid and penetrating. Amy shivered. It felt as if ghosts were flying up her nostrils. She pulled a copy of the poem from her back pocket and held it near the light. "'Deep within Gurkhani Zij / Lies Taragai's unfinished prize: / The unperfected instrument, / Though vast in power, small in size'—that's our first hint. The astrolabe is a small instrument. Jake and I are thinking it's hidden here somewhere."

Her voice echoed eerily. She imagined it floating out of the observatory and over the graves, amusing the dead. "Keep the volume down," she added.

"What's the next part?" Dan whispered, peering at the poem. "'What of this work of Ulugh Beg, / Who dared to count infinity? / His catalog, though vast in scope / Yet of divisions had but three.'"

"His catalog of stars numbered one thousand eighteen," Jake said. "But that can only be divided into two numbers—two and five hundred nine."

Amy stepped to the top of the stairs leading down the sextant. She pulled aside a rope gate and said softly, "We never got a chance to look closely at the walls. That was where he recorded the stars. Maybe the numbers are there."

She descended the sextant steps, looking closely for the numbers two and five hundred nine. Jake fell in quickly behind her, shining the light on the wall. "Amy, the stuff eroded away long ago. There's nothing here."

Amy nodded. He was right. "Read the rest of the poem, Dan," she said.

Without any light, Dan recited, "'When listed in descending rank, / The Fakhri apex as a start, / Descend and rise, descend again, / And stand thee o'er my ruler's heart.'"

"How do you know that?" Jake asked.

"Good memory," Dan replied.

"'Descend and rise'!" Atticus exclaimed. "Like the sun or the moon! Is there any kind of sun or moon symbol you can recognize?"

"Ssssh." Amy grabbed the flashlight from Jake and began shining it around.

"Guys?" Dan said, walking down the steps. "The sun and the moon are not the only things here that rise and descend."

"The stairs!" Atticus exclaimed. "Dan, that's amazing. Maybe those numbers mean *the number of steps*!"

"But there aren't five hundred and nine steps," Amy said.

Atticus frowned. "Oh."

Amy thought hard. One aspect of the poem was

bugging her. "I don't get something. Why does the poem say, 'of divisions, had but *three*' — when it's obvious the number of stars has only two factors?"

"Maybe division was done differently back then?" Dan said.

"Or maybe the number of stars is wrong," Jake surmised.

Amy nodded. "Yes. When we went on that tour — didn't Umarov say there were other scholars, other estimations . . ."

"One thousand twenty-two!" Dan shot back.

"What?" Jake said.

Dan's fingers were pressed to his forehead. "Trying to remember . . . His exact words were 'Well, some scholars say one thousand twenty-two, but who's counting?' Yes, that's it! Try that number!"

Atticus let out a whoop. "That is an *awesome* memory!"

"SSSHHH!" Amy said, shoving the flashlight under her chin and pulling out her smartphone. In a moment, she had the answer:

```
1,022 = 2 x 7 x 73
```

"Three prime factors," she said.

Amy quickly read the last section of the poem:

"When listed in descending rank,
The Fakhri apex as a start,

Descend and rise, descend again,
And stand thee o'er my ruler's heart."

"Descending rank," she said. "So we start from the highest number — meaning seventy-three first. . . ."

"The Fakhri apex would be the top," Jake said. "But the left or the right?"

"Try them both!" Amy replied. "Down seventy-three, up seven, down two."

"Atticus and I will do it!" Dan grabbed the flashlight. As he and Atticus descended the left side, they began counting the steps. Seventy-three got them to the bottom. They rose seven steps, then descended two. "Now what?" Dan murmured.

Jake and Amy raced down to meet them. Amy knelt. She noticed the steps were actually made of small, oblong stones — like piano keys, or fingers. She pulled on each one. Jake sidled to the right side and pulled on those.

"They're solid," Amy said. "This is hopeless."

"Atticus — I need the light!" Jake cried out. His neck was bulging as he pulled on one of the stones. "I . . . think . . . this one's loose. . . ."

Atticus put the flashlight down, angling it so it illuminated the stone. He knelt beside his brother and pulled. Amy joined them.

The stone didn't budge.

As Amy was about to let go, a low thrumming sound began. At first, she thought it was her own stomach rumbling. Then she felt her body shift. Rocks began to rain down from the wall.

"Whoa . . ." Dan gasped.

In the center of the track, between the two long ribbons of curved stone, a trap door was opening. Two massive stones moved apart diagonally from each other, like hands pivoting at the wrists.

Amy fell back. She scrambled toward the center, gazing down into the hole.

Utter blackness.

Now Jake was beside her, shining the flashlight. It caught the edge of a large box, blackened with soot and dirt. "What the heck is this?"

Together they pulled upward, but the box wouldn't fit through. Atticus dug into his pocket and pulled out a Swiss Army knife. He wedged the can opener under the top of box and pulled upward. With a loud *squawk*, the top pulled off.

Amy reached inside and wrapped her fingers around a thick disc of heavy, solid brass. As she lifted it out, Jake shone the light on its fretwork of finely tooled metal. Complex symbols were carved on the outer rim, and on the inside were circular patterns and intricate designs. Through the middle ran a lever like a clock hand, attached at the center.

"It's like a giant watch," Jake said.

"This is the thing Ulugh Beg thought would match the power of the sextant?" Dan asked.

"This is the thing Vesper One wants," Amy replied.

She looked at her watch. 10:31. "Nineteen minutes! We beat the deadline!"

"No! No, we didn't!" Dan was racing up the stairs.

"What's wrong, Dan?" Amy called out.

Dan held up his phone. Even in the dark, his eyes shone with fear. "I have zero bars."

Amy's insides lurched. If they had no reception, Vesper One wouldn't be able to reach them. He wouldn't know they found the astrolabe.

Cradling the instrument, she bolted up the stairs.

Jake barreled past her. At the top, he yanked Dan back. Whirling him around, he put his finger to his lips.

A voice crackled outside. "What's that?" Amy whispered.

Jake forced Dan's shaking hand to shine the flash-light on his face.

He mouthed one word.

Police!

CHAPTER 26

Dan switched off the light. The voices were quickly coming closer. Amy could hear the crunch of gravel beneath footsteps. "What are they saying?" she asked.

"How sh-should I know?" Dan hissed. "I don't speak Uzbek!"

"Get back!" Jake whispered.

Dan looked terrified. "B-but . . . *Uncle Alistair* . . . !"

"Get to the bottom—now!" Jake shoved him. Dan's hurtling body nearly toppled Amy, but they both managed to climb to the bottom with Atticus.

Jake was still on the stairs—and now he was climbing!

"Ja—!" Amy started to yell, but Atticus clamped his hand over her mouth.

His footfalls echoed loudly. Outside, voices were coming nearer.

Amy tried to run up after him, but both Dan and Atticus pulled her back. "He'll get hurt!" she whispered.

"He knows what he's doing," Atticus replied firmly. "If he told us to stay, that's the best advice."

Now the tunnel ceiling was coming to life with reflected flashlights. It seemed like a cruel imitation of the night sky, a mockery of Ulugh Beg's precise measurements.

Voices rose as men entered. They were yelling at Jake in Uzbek, and as he answered in English, Amy could make out words: *police . . . trespass . . . arrest . . .*

Footsteps came closer to the railing over their heads. "There's no one else!" Jake was saying. "Just me!"

But now a flashlight beam was swinging down the rutted wall, outlining the steps on the other side. . . .

"Come back here!" a thick-accented voice bellowed from above, booming through the vast tunnel.

Suddenly, the lights were gone. Footsteps were racing away, out the door again. Amy heard Jake's voice yelling, but the sound was outside.

Jake had run off, slipped away.

"He's creating a distraction," Amy said. "Let's go!"

The railing area above, crowded a moment earlier, was now empty. Amy took the steps three at a time. At the top, she ran for the door and carefully peered out.

Jake had somehow made his way across the plateau. An officer had caught him by the collar and was slamming him against a car. There were two cars, four officers, all of them with their backs turned.

Amy's breath caught in her throat. She fought the urge to run after him. But she knew that would only ruin what he'd set out to do.

Jake was taking one for the team now.

For Uncle Alistair.

Amy turned. Silently she pointed toward the far end of the plateau, away from the driveway. And she ran.

Atticus and Dan followed her to the edge. In the dark, all she could see was a sharp drop-off.

Amy glanced over her shoulder. The frame of the sextant's entrance blocked them from the sight of the police. Dan flicked on his flashlight and shone it downward. The light traced a steep, rockstrewn path.

"Come on." Amy clutched the delicate tool to her chest and stepped off. Her heel dug into the gravelly slope. With a loud *sssshh*, it slid about a foot. She let out a squeal.

"Go . . . *go!*" Dan said.

She carefully lifted her other foot and set it down sideways, trying to keep her balance. The gravel slipped again, and this time the ground gave way beneath her.

Amy's back scraped against the soil. Her head hit it and then bounced back. She was sliding, head over heels, her arms hugging the instrument tightly.

"*Amy!*" Dan shouted, tumbling after her.

They collided at the bottom. Amy smashed backward into the trunk of a scraggly tree.

"Yeow!" came a cry to their left. Atticus.

Amy unfolded herself. Her chest throbbed. In the morning, it would have an indentation of the astrolabe.

She glanced at her watch — 10:49. "Dan?" she cried out. "How many bars?"

His eyes were as bright as a supernova. "Two!"

One minute left. Vesper One could reach them now. He was a stickler for promptness. Amy looked up. The police voices were coming closer.

"They must have heard us," Atticus whispered.

Amy scrambled behind the thin trunk of an olive tree.

"Ow!" came Jake's voice from above. "I twisted my ankle. I'll sue! You're going to hear from my lawyer!"

An eerie beep pierced the night air. Amy stiffened.

Dan's phone glowed with a message. "He's early."

```
I've been waiting to hear from you. After
all, you have the ability to contact me,
don't you? Counting the seconds . . .
```

"We have to use Luna's phone!" Dan whispered.

Atticus's face was a rictus of fear. "We have twenty seconds!"

Amy dropped the astrolabe. She fumbled in her pocket for the phone.

It was gone. "I don't have it!"

"What?" Dan shot back. "What did you do with it?"

"I don't know!" Amy grabbed the flashlight from her brother and shone it around the area. She didn't care if the police saw it.

There. She had nearly missed the glint of metal at the base of the drop-off. The phone must have fallen from her pocket when she landed.

She scrambled to it but Dan got there first.

"One second!" Atticus said.

"Hurry!" Amy urged.

Dan hit REDIAL. He thumbed two words—

```
Got it
```

But his finger slipped on the way to the SEND key, typing another character.

```
Got it1
```

"Time's up!" Atticus shouted.

"Press send, Dan—*send!*" Amy said.

"There!" Dan shouted, showing her the screen.

```
Sending . . .
```

Above them, the beam of light scanned the area. It swept across the tree where they'd just been. Amy, Dan, and Atticus pressed their bodies against the edge of the cliff.

Amy's eyes did not waver from the screen.

The lights above them went away. The sound of shutting car doors punctuated the night. Then the dull roar of two car engines.

But the screen remained blank.

10:51.

"It can't be. . . ." Dan shook the phone. "Something must be wrong."

It couldn't be. A slip of the finger. A microscopic bead of sweat causing him to press 1 instead of SEND.

"It's my fault," Amy moaned. "I didn't mean to drop the phone."

"I don't care!" Dan said. *"I just want to know what happened to Uncle Alistair!"*

"That guy—Vesper One—he couldn't have," Atticus said. "He wouldn't. . . ."

Dan wheeled on him. "Oh, yes, he would. And you know what? I will return the favor some day. I will kill him." He raised his face to the sky. *"Did you hear me? I will kill you, AJT!"*

"Dan—?" Amy said.

"I know what you're going to say, Amy," Dan said through a torrent of tears, "but I hate him. I hate our—"

"No, look!" Amy said, pointing to the phone in his hand. "Your screen just lit up!"

The phone had turned liquid in Dan's vision. He blinked and focused on the words:

```
Did I scare you? Don't let it be said I
don't have a sense of drama.

And since you like the illusion of control,
I will make the drop easy. Someone is
coming to you.

Oh, yes. Congratulations. Your dear uncle
is safe.

For now.
```

As the police car lurched, Jake Rosenbloom tried not to get carsick. "Where are you taking me?" he asked.

One of the officers in the front seat turned to face him. "You were trespassing. Resisting arrest. We must file report."

Jake slumped into the seat. He hoped that Dan and Amy had been able to make the drop.

The driver muttered something in Uzbek and yanked the steering wheel to the right. Another car had fishtailed and was now broadside across both lanes.

With a screech of tires, the car swerved off the road and into a ditch. Jake braced himself. Even though he was wearing a seat belt, his face smashed against the side window.

The police leaped out of the car, yelling at the top of their lungs. Guns drawn, they approached the other car. It was a long, black limo with dark windows.

Jake grimaced, reaching up to touch a gash on the side of his head. Blood trickled down his cheek. Too early to know how serious this was. But he felt okay. More or less.

He glanced back outside and saw the limo's back window rolling down. Inside was a man wearing a black hat and sunglasses. He looked up slowly at the cops and shrugged, as if to say he didn't understand. Which only made the cops shout louder.

Jake looked to the right. It was nearly pitch-black. He slid over to that side of the car and tried the door. It swung open.

He knew he didn't have much time. He jumped out of the car, tumbling into the small ditch. A few yards beyond it was an open gate. He stood. His head throbbed, but he was mobile.

He raced through the gate at top speed.

Behind him came two quick shouts, then silence.

And the thudding of heavy footsteps in pursuit.

The sunrise came as a shock. Amy realized she had no sense of day and night anymore. It seemed only moments ago that Vesper One's message had come through:

Change of plans. At the earliest light, enter the graveyard. Use the entrance near the Shah-i-Zindi, just before the Siab Dekhkhan Bazaar. At precisely 5:30 a.m., find Olga Sakarov by the base of the nearest hill. And say hi from me.

As she entered the graveyard, the tombstones looked like lost, frozen souls, glowing with a pale silver light.

She clutched tightly to the astrolabe, tilting her wrist to check her watch. 5:15. They were fifteen minutes away from the drop. Acting, as always, on Vesper One's instructions. *Like puppets,* she thought.

"Let's move," Amy said.

Fiddling with his phone, Atticus nearly stumbled.

"Any luck?" whispered Dan.

"No response from Jake," Atticus said, his voice thick with emotion. "I've been trying for six hours."

Amy looked left and right as she edged into the pathway. Her neck ached. Sleeping in the field had not been comfy. She and Dan had managed some uncomfortable shut-eye, but she was worried about Atticus. He hadn't slept at all.

"I don't see our contact person," Dan said.

"Maybe it's the wrong place for the drop," Atticus suggested.

Dan angled the screen toward him. Amy stopped to read the message once again.

"Olga Sakarov . . . she even sounds like a Vesper," Dan said.

A small animal skittered across Amy's path. She stifled a scream, took a deep breath, and stepped carefully. Polished stone slabs of all shapes rose around her like road signs. They were etched with faces that seemed to glower with disapproval.

"These names are in Cyrillic," Atticus said.

"They look like real stone to me," Dan remarked.

"*Cyrillic*, not *acrylic*," Atticus said. "It's the Russian alphabet. Samarkand has a huge Russian population."

Amy stopped at the foot of the hill. The distant birdsong sounded like screams of the dying. As the sun's crown oozed over the horizon, a vulture hovered overhead. Amy checked her watch. 5:24. "She should be within sight by now."

"She better get here before that thing gets us," Dan said.

"It's a vulture," Atticus said. "They only eat carrion. Dead animals."

Out of the corner of her eye, Amy spotted another small critter racing across the ground. It stopped just beyond a massive gravestone, near a soft, ragged lump on the ground. It looked like a freshly killed squirrel. "There's its breakfast," Amy said.

Dan was walking closer to the lump, squinting. He stopped and turned, his face pale. "It's not the only dead thing."

Amy followed his glance to the silhouette of a foot, sticking out from behind the tombstone.

Atticus gasped.

"Is that . . . Olga?" Dan whispered.

Amy moved closer, girding herself against her worst fear. That Vesper One had found a total stranger and killed her. Just for kicks. As a warning.

A hostage by proxy.

Overhead came an angry cawing. *Move away and let nature take its course. Leave the dead for the living.* Every instinct told Amy to run from this creepy scene. Just drop the astrolabe and run.

"The foot . . ." Atticus said, holding tight to Amy's arm. "It's too wide for an Olga."

Amy could see a leg now, wearing jeans. "H-h-hello?" she called out.

Dreading what she would see, she came around the front of the stone. A young man was sprawled on the grass, his head angled back into a shadow.

She stepped forward to see his face.

"Jake?"

CHAPTER 28

The first thing Jake Rosenbloom realized upon awakening was that it was raining. The second was that something was screeching high above.

The third was that the rain was actually Amy Cahill crying into his face. "Jake, you're alive!"

Jake sat forward. He felt as if someone had split his head open with a pickax. "I hope so," he said.

"Oh, man, I thought I would never see you. . . ." Now Atticus was hugging him, sobbing. "What happened?"

"I'm not sure . . . it was confusing. . . ." Jake touched his head and immediately jumped from the pain.

"We should have faced the police together," Dan said. "If we had, the Vespers would have taken the astrolabe. That's all they wanted to do."

"So why don't they just take it now and leave us alone?" Atticus asked, looking around the cemetery. "Where are they?"

"I don't know," Amy said, reaching down to help Jake up. "They told us to meet someone here at exactly five-thirty. Olga Sakarov."

Jake groaned as he rose. He blinked his eyes, taking in the surroundings.

And suddenly he understood.

Although he had made a commitment to the Cahills, he hadn't fully appreciated what they were up against. As he looked at Amy, he could read the lines on her face. They traced out a map of trouble, an old person's pain on someone only sixteen. The Cahills, he knew, were in a hole so deep there might be no way out. A hole that he and his brother were in now, too.

He had never felt so right about his decision to join Dan and Amy in the fight against the Vespers. "They did this to me," Jake said, "to teach you a lesson."

He stood away from the tombstone behind him so that the others could see:

Ольга Сахарова
1964 – 1997

Atticus swallowed hard. "Olga Sakarov."

"She was a prop," Jake said. "A symbol of what could happen to any of us. He put me here, noted the name, and texted you. A morbid scene he wanted you to see."

He looked at Amy's watch. 5:30.

A loud scream rang out overhead. All four of them craned their necks upward.

The vulture, which had been hovering hungrily, was now flying away. Swooping down from the sky, its wings spread wide, was another creature — a thick-bodied raptor with a long neck and a sharp beak.

"Move!" Amy said. "It's going after the dead meat!"

They scrambled back the way they came. With a tilt of its body, the bird followed. As it neared Amy, it opened its talons and let out a chittering squeal.

"Amyyyyy!" Dan was yelling.

Amy screamed. There was a brush of feathers against her hair. Talons clamped solidly on the astrolabe and pulled upward.

Amy felt the disc lift out of her clutches. The hawk soared into the rising sun, the astrolabe hanging like a helpless animal.

Amy raced to the top of the hill to watch. The bird was descending now, toward a distant road.

There, the solid black window of a black limousine rolled down. A leather-gloved hand reached out toward the sky, palm up.

The bird dropped fast, braking its descent just short of the car. The hand reached out, grabbed the astrolabe, and pulled it into the window.

Now Amy could see a man with sunglasses inside. He was blowing them all a kiss.

CHAPTER 29

Sinead looked like she was going to jump through the laptop screen. "Amy, you are a hero!"

"Um . . . just *Amy*?" Dan said.

Amy stuck out her tongue at him. Cackling, Dan flopped back on the stone bench outside the Shah-i-Zindi mosque and watched the sun playing on the turquoise tiles. The place was quiet enough—and private enough—for a link to Attleboro.

"Well, everyone helped," Amy said. "Atticus figured out the final code. Jake nearly sacrificed his life. And Dan . . . let me think. . . ."

Amy braced herself for a protest. But instead, Dan seemed preoccupied with his phone. "Guys . . ." he said. "We've got confirmation."

He held his phone up to Amy, Atticus, and Jake—and then to the screen, for Sinead to see.

```
The drop was lovely. Many thanks to all
who made it possible. Including dear Olga
Sakarov.
```

Well, time to celebrate. And what better place than the cheerful city of Berlin? Home of a priceless jewel, in a heavily guarded museum. I trust you have heard of it. Because your next assignment is to liberate it. And deliver it to me.

Thanks in advance. And a jolly "Guten tag!" from Uncle Alistair.

"Germany?" Jake said. "Why? And what jewel?"

Dan shrugged. "Let Amy do the research. She likes that part."

"I wish Vesper One wouldn't joke about Uncle Alistair like that," Sinead said.

Amy nodded. "I've been thinking about him all day. About what he avoided."

"Thanks to all of you," Sinead said. Her eyes darted left. "Um, Evan and I do have some news to report."

Evan leaned into the screen. "Sinead and I are friends again. She totally nailed the lizard. Well, not actually impaled it with a nail. I mean, the identity of the lizard. And its type. Which is actually given away by its name, funnily enough—"

"Your brilliant guardian Nellie," Sinead said, "was holding up an Argentine giant tegu."

Amy nearly leaped off the bench. "Argentina! That's amazing data. You pinpointed it!"

"Yesss!" Dan shouted.

Sinead eyed Evan, then turned back to the screen. "I've also been running a trace on Ian. We have confirmation he visited his mother. The good news is that he wasn't kidnapped. The bad news is that immediately after seeing her, he changed his flight."

"He's in Argentina, Amy," Evan said.

"Which also happens to be the location of one of Isabel Kabra's strongholds," Sinead added.

Amy rocked back on the bench. *Isabel.* Was she the master kidnapper? Could she be Vesper One? "Ian must have found out about the hostages' location," she said. "From his mother. And he went straight there."

"Without contacting us?" Sinead said with an exasperated sigh. "He's off the Cahill grid, Amy. Total radio silence."

"I never did trust that guy," Evan said. "I mean, with all respect."

Amy shook her head. This didn't add up. Ian couldn't be involved with the Vespers. He was every bit as strong a Cahill as Sinead and Evan were. "Give him some time . . ." she said.

"We have our people on the case, inspecting every lead . . ." Evan said, his voice trailing off. "Um, Amy? Are you okay?"

Amy's eyes were misting. "I'm fine. Thanks, Evan. For all the amazing work. You're the best."

"Somebody cue the violins," Dan said.

"Uh, sounds to me as if Sinead is actually the

one who deserves the thanks," Jake said.

Evan arched his eyebrows at the remark. "Amy Cahill is the head of the family. She can think for herself."

Another airport. Another flight. Another delay.

At least this one had a good gift shop. With a collection of small aloe plants.

Seventeen ingredients.

Progress.

Dan sank against the wall, near a group of backpackers from Germany. Three flights were leaving from the same gate, and already two had been canceled.

Amy and Jake were off to get food. Atticus was sacked out against the opposite wall. Snoring.

Cautiously he snapped open his phone and read the message that had come in from AJT.

```
Hello, Dan! Figured maybe you had some
downtime. Contact me when you want.
Patience is my middle name. Just ignore
the J. :)
```

The tone was so appalling, Dan nearly laughed.

He'd murdered Mr. McIntyre. He'd had Jake beaten up in a graveyard . . . as a stunt!

What would he have done if I hadn't pressed SEND in time to save Uncle Alistair?

Dan wanted to throw the phone under the wheels of a jumbo jet. Hire a hypnotist to wipe the memory of the messages from his brain.

But the feeling was back.

Against all odds, against every atom of human reason, the message gave him a strange sensation. A tingling from the bottom of his toes. Something like hope.

Bordering on insanity.

He snapped the phone shut and stuck it in his pocket. Then he closed his eyes, counted to ten, and opened them.

He took several deep breaths. He reminded himself that he was hungry. He pulled a squashed candy bar from his backpack and began to unwrap it. Each of these things was calming him down.

"'Allo?" said one of the Germans, a rosy-cheeked girl about Dan's age.

"Hello," Dan said.

"You have 'allo?" the girl persisted, pointing inside the pack—to a green leaf that was jutting out of a plastic bag.

"Oh, *aloe*?" Dan said. "Yup. To . . . um, to rub on my—"

"Sunburn." The girl pulled down the collar of her T-shirt to reveal a patch of bright red skin below her collarbone.

"TMI . . ." Dan murmured, quickly breaking off a piece of the leaf and giving it to her. "Okay? Auf Wiedersehen. Whatever. Gotta book."

He shoved the candy bar in his mouth and found

a seat under a picture window. Rain pounded on the glass.

He had to be more careful about hiding the ingredients. One glance at the aloe plant, and Amy would know.

Overhead, a news report blared on an airport TV monitor. There was a report about a father and a little boy finding each other after a tornado. They were grinning, and they looked so much like each other.

Like twins, separated by a generation . . .

Amy's words echoed in his brain. *When you were little, he'd hold you up to everyone and say, 'Moon face!' You both would flash this big, identical grin.*

Dan sat bolt upright.

Of course. He could settle the AJT problem once and for all. Why hadn't he thought of this before? No stranger could possibly know that fact.

He checked left and right, then opened the phone again. This time he composed a message and sent it right away:

```
If you're really my dad, can you tell me
what special thing you said to make us
smile together?
```

The answer came back far faster than he would have expected.

```
Moon face.
```

HELLO CAHILLS!

Do you ever feel that you lack a certain sparkle? I do. In fact, right now I lack exactly 545.67 carats worth of sparkle. Get the Jubilee for me and I'm sure I'll feel better. And don't make me say pretty please. I doubt you'll like the consequences.

Vesper One